LOVE OR MONEY?

"Where have you been?" she asked.

"Poking around, maybe where I shouldn't look."

"What are you saying?" She sat beside him on the small settee, her leg pressing against his. Slocum found it harder to think when Grace was this close.

"I wanted to ask about the bank and your uncle."

"Business," Grace said, sighing deeply. He couldn't help noticing the way her breasts rose and fell under the crisp white blouse. In deference to the heat, she wore nothing under the linen. He saw how her nipples pressed into the fabric, telling him where her thoughts were.

"Later," he said as he put his arms around her.

DON'T MISS THESE
ALL-ACTION WESTERN SERIES
FROM THE BERKLEY PUBLISHING GROUP

THE GUNSMITH by J. R. Roberts
Clint Adams was a legend among lawmen, outlaws, and ladies.
They called him . . . the Gunsmith.

LONGARM by Tabor Evans
The popular long-running series about U.S. Deputy Marshal
Long—his life, his loves, his fight for justice.

SLOCUM by Jake Logan
Today's longest-running action Western. John Slocum rides
a deadly trail of hot blood and cold steel.

BUSHWHACKERS by B. J. Lanagan
An action-packed series by the creators of Longarm! The
rousing adventures of the most brutal gang of cutthroats ever
assembled—Quantrill's Raiders.

DIAMONDBACK by Guy Brewer
Dex Yancey is Diamondback, a southern gentleman turned
con man when his brother cheats him out of the family fortune. Ladies love him. Gamblers hate him. But nobody pulls
one over on Dex . . .

WILDGUN by Jack Hanson
Will Barlow's continuing search for his daughter, kidnapped
by the Blackfeet Indians who slaughtered the rest of his family.

JAKE LOGAN

SLOCUM AND THE GILA RANGERS

J

JOVE BOOKS, NEW YORK

SLOCUM AND THE GILA RANGERS

A Jove Book / published by arrangement with the author

PRINTING HISTORY
Jove edition / October 2000

The Penguin Putnam Inc. World Wide Web site address is
http://www.penguinputnam.com

ISBN: 0-515-12931-3

A JOVE BOOK®
Jove Books are published by The Berkley Publishing Group,
a division of Penguin Putnam Inc.,
375 Hudson Street, New York, New York 10014.
JOVE and the "J" design
are trademarks belonging to Penguin Putnam Inc.

PRINTED IN THE UNITED STATES OF AMERICA

10 9 8 7 6 5 4 3 2 1

1

"How much you got, Slocum?" Clay Tolliver pulled down the rim of his floppy black hat and peered at John Slocum, sizing him up. The tall, rangy man grinned his lopsided grin, and seemed almost happy at the prospect of worming the answer out of Slocum. It was about as much fun as either of them had enjoyed in the past week or two.

"About as much as you," Slocum reluctantly replied. He did not have to paw through his shirt pockets for change. There wasn't any left. He had spent his last silver dollar two days ago, buying more ammunition from a stationmaster along the Gila Road, used almost exclusively by the Butterfield Stagecoach Company in this part of southern Arizona. Nobody but coach drivers, Gila monsters, and fools ventured out in this deadly inferno.

The way his belly complained, he wished now he had bought a can of peaches or a bag of dried pinto beans instead of the ammunition. Slocum had thought to hunt along the road, but even rabbits were scarce in the scorching midsummer heat.

Tolliver took off his hat, mopped at the sweat beading his wrinkled forehead, then pulled the hat back down squarely so it rested on the tops of his big ears. He tied the bandanna back around his neck to protect his flesh from the burning Arizona sun.

"Wrong," Tolliver said. "I got less."

"I don't have anything. How can you have less than nothing?" asked Slocum.

"I owe you two dollars I ain't got, that's how." Tolliver laughed. "Maybe that means *you* are worse off since you ain't gonna collect. Not unless some rich relative I don't have up and dies, leavin' his entire fortune to me."

Slocum had to smile. He had been partners with Tolliver for more than three months. They had ridden some hard trails together, and he had found himself liking the tall, whipsaw-muscled cowboy more and more. Tolliver's sense of humor grated on Slocum's nerves at times, but when the cowboy had come to realize how little Slocum liked practical jokes, he had stopped. But the other jokes came like a flood at times, lightening the dark mood that so often seized Slocum and held him in its grip like some rabid bulldog.

"No jobs. Never seen ranchers so closed in on themselves," Slocum said. "Can't even drift south of the border and work on a hacienda. The *vaqueros* are worse off than we are."

"The heat, the drought, the inhumanity of man against man," Tolliver said philosophically. He spat. The gob came out thick, and sizzled when it hit a flat rock next to where they sat, looking down the Butterfield Stage line. To the west were only a few pitiful mud huts that passed as way stations. Slocum was not certain what lay to the east, but it had to be better. If the world suddenly fell off into nothingness, *that* was better.

"Something's eating at you," Slocum said. "What is it?"

"Well, Slocum, it's like this. We been together a spell but only doin' legit work."

"We were both busting broncos for Pills Paulsen," Slocum agreed. Doc Paulsen had been a medical doctor turned ranch owner in serious need of hands to work his spread up near Flagstaff. Slocum had drifted in from up north, and Tolliver had just been there. The two of them had done more to help out Paulsen than any ten men in his employ.

Truth was, if things had been different, Slocum wouldn't have minded working for Pills Paulsen a spell longer. Fate had dealt another hand, though. The doctor had been kicked in the head by one of the unbroken horses, lapsed into a coma, and died a week later. Slocum was never quite sure what went on after that, but it seemed that two bankers and a couple others waving official papers had swooped down like carrion birds and had gobbled up the ranch, divvying it among themselves.

Slocum and Tolliver had started south, passing through scorched Yuma and then east across the Sonoran Desert, past the peculiar San Carlos River, which ran north to south, and had ended up in the middle of nowhere, without money or prospects.

"Well, I done more 'n my day than breakin' horses," Tolliver said, his bright blue eyes fixed on Slocum's green ones. The man pushed back his hat again, revealing the leathery, honest face and the nose that had been straight before being broken one time too many.

"What are you telling me?"

"I robbed a bank or two in my time," Tolliver said. "Might be a wanted poster out on me. Might not either. It's been a long time."

Slocum said nothing. Tolliver was a nervy one, but this declaration of illegal indiscretion did not surprise him too much. He had crossed the line more than a few times himself. At the end of the war, he had recuperated from being gutshot by his own commander and had returned to Slocum's Stand in Calhoun, Georgia. His parents were dead and his only brother, Robert, had died at Gettysburg.

Slocum touched the pocket watch that was his only legacy from Robert.

He owned that spread in the green, gentle hills of Georgia, but the carpetbagger judge had other ideas. No taxes had been paid, the crooked judge said. When he and a gunman rode out to take possession, Slocum was not inclined to argue. Two fresh graves popped up on the hill by the springhouse, and Slocum had ridden on, a warrant for judge-killing dogging his steps ever since.

In some ways, this had been the least of his crimes against society. He had lived a hard life, and made no excuses for what he had done to stay alive.

"I'm not lily-white myself," Slocum said with typical understatement.

"Didn't think so," Tolliver said, heaving a sigh of relief. He pointed to the stage road. "I been thinkin' 'bout that road."

"Stage-robbing is risky business. There's no telling what they'll be carrying, unless we had inside information, and more than once a passenger takes it into his head to come out with six-guns blazing."

"Naw, Slocum, I ain't thinkin' on a stage. You go where the stage does."

"A town?"

"A town with a bank. Now that road's got to lead somewhere sometime. We keep on, we find the town and rob the bank. Don't matter much what we haul out since it's bound to be more 'n we got now."

"I'm not saying yes," Slocum said, getting to his feet and dusting himself off.

"But you're not sayin' no, are you?" Tolliver grinned, the blazing sunlight glinting off a gold tooth in the front of his mouth.

"Nope."

Tolliver whooped in glee and started down the trail, leading his horse. Slocum followed close behind, wondering if he was making a bad mistake. It was good to know the men riding into a robbery, and Slocum knew he could trust Clay Tolliver not to abandon him if things went wrong, but he had a feeling in his gut this was not right.

Worse than the uneasy feeling, Slocum could not put his finger on the reason for it.

"What a town," Clay Tolliver marveled, shaking his head as he looked down the main street of Neutral, Arizona. "Must be a saloon for every other cowpoke."

Slocum saw nothing out of place with that. This was a boomtown on its last legs. There had been gold mines in the hills above Neutral that were petering out. Money still flowed down this street, but nowhere near what there had been even a few months earlier, if he was any judge.

Still, Neutral was prosperous and the bank in its adobe building looked secure. Maybe too secure.

"The biggest mine's closed," Slocum said. "That means no payroll being stashed in the bank."

"But the other mine owners have their dough there," Tolliver pointed out. "Where else would they put it?"

"Into property, into saloons and gambling and women," Slocum said.

"Naw, Slocum, you don't know how them rich folks think. If Neutral is on the skids, they'll be pullin' their money out and puttin' it in San Francisco or Denver or even someplace with better prospects. They won't buy property. They'll *sell* it. And that money's sittin' purty in that there bank."

"First Bank of Arizona Territory" read the weather-beaten sign on the building sitting by itself at the end of the long and dusty main street. Slocum nodded as he considered what Tolliver said. His partner had a good mind. The men with money would be funneling it through this bank to places with better pickings.

However, the bank had a sturdy look to it that worried Slocum. Adobe walls close to five feet thick would take forever to dig through if he and Tolliver tried to sneak in after hours. That meant they had to go in with guns drawn and ready to kill someone, if there were guards or tellers with more guts than brains.

"We won't have to blow the vault," Tolliver pointed out. "We waltz right on in, purty as you please, and have the bank president open his safe for us."

"That's an expensive building for these parts. There must be guards."

"Reckon so," Tolliver allowed. "Let's you and me go on in and see."

Slocum had no objection. Sooner or later they had to enter the bank to scout all the details. Why not now?

Tolliver stopped dead in his tracks in the middle of the street. For the first time he looked apprehensive about their proposed crime.

"What we going to say if they ask why we're in there?"

"We're sure not going to tell them we're opening an account," Slocum said. This made Tolliver laugh. "Ask about guard jobs. We look the role."

"Yeah, a good idea, Slocum. You think fast. That's good, real good." The closer they got to the double doors leading into the bank, the more nervous Tolliver became. Slocum was worried that the man might draw too much attention.

Already a short, sturdily built man near the door was eying them curiously. The man worked a mite at twirling the tips of his mustache. For all his attention to the hair on his upper lip, he stood with his feet apart a ways and an air about him that said he knew how to use the two six-shooters shoved into his broad, hand-tooled Mexican leather belt.

"Go on around back and see if there is any way we might get in without causing a ruckus," Slocum told Tolliver. The man hurried off, glad not to be part of the actual scouting. Slocum paused a moment, wondering about the man by the door.

The man nodded brusquely to him and walked off, bowed legs almost comical as he went down the street toward the Snake Eyes Saloon and Dance Hall. Slocum waited until the mustached man vanished before going into the bank. Whether Tolliver was spooking Slocum needlessly, he did not know. The mustached man had never bothered glancing back once he had left the bank's front door.

Slocum stepped from the burning heat of midday into the cool, dim interior. The sudden difference in temperature caused him to shiver. His eyes worked hard to adjust to the lower level of light, and he stepped to one side as much to size up the bank lobby as to be able to see.

Barely had he taken a step when two men burst through the front door. One shoved him aside so hard he staggered and fell, catching himself against the dusty inner adobe wall of the bank.

"This is a holdup!" bellowed the masked man who had pushed him aside. "Don't nobody go and be a hero now, you hear?"

Slocum half turned, keeping the Colt Navy in its cross-draw holster hidden from the robbers. Six men crowded in, all wearing bandannas and waving around firearms. Two carried sawed-off shotguns. The rest held six-guns.

Slocum had faced men with drawn guns before and not been afraid. Now a spark of fear coursed through him. The pair with the shotguns were wild cards, nervous, jerky, obviously unused to robbing banks. That made them worse than blobs of nitroglycerine sitting in the hot sun. Jostle them a mite and they'd go off unexpectedly.

"Get those drawers empty, you hear?" bellowed the one Slocum pegged to be the leader. "Where's the president of this here bank?"

"H-he's in the back room," stammered a teller, not sure whether to keep his hands high or to clean out the cash drawer when a robber shoved a pillowcase at him.

"Get him out here. Now!"

Slocum blinked in surprise. From the back room he assumed to be the president's office came about the loveliest woman he had set eyes on in years. Tall, proud, shoulders back, head high and chin thrust out defiantly, she was a vision of beauty. Her green eyes flashed angrily, and she tossed her long, flowing mane of coppery red hair like a frisky filly.

"What is the meaning of this?" she demanded.

"Shut up," the leader said. "Is the banker in there?" He pointed with his six-shooter. The woman pushed it aside.

"Yes," she said, staring him down. Slocum saw right away such bravado was a bad idea. The robber swung his six-shooter back and pointed it directly between her eyes. He drew back the hammer, cocking the pistol. The robber's trigger finger turned white as he squeezed back.

For the first time the woman realized how close to death she was.

"I came here to see him. Don't go doing anything that'll make him turn down my loan!" Slocum called out. He broke the spell of killing fury that had seized the robber.

The man swung on him, the six-shooter aimed at Slocum rather than the woman now.

"You shut your pie hole, mister," snapped the robber.

"We 'bout got all the cash," piped up another of the robbers. "Let's get the hell out of here!"

"Not till we empty that vault. This is chicken feed compared to what's stashed in there." The robber shifted the six-shooter from Slocum to indicate the looming black-faced Chubb safe in the other room at the rear of the bank. The twin doors were securely locked, if Slocum was any judge.

And the robber was likely to kill people to get it open. Of that Slocum had not a speck of doubt.

"Don't you go harassing my daughter like that," blustered a portly man of medium height coming from the president's office. From the way he was dressed so elegantly—the diamond-headlight stickpin, the shiny shoes, and the dangling gold watch chain sporting the emblem of the Masonic Lodge—this had to be the banker.

"Yer daughter? How'd an ugly galoot like you end up with a pretty little thing like her? Are you adopted?" The robber reached out and brushed his fingers over the woman's cheek. She rared back as if she was going to slap him. The banker moved to interpose himself between his daughter and the robber.

"Get out of here! Immediately. Sheriff Hardeen will—"

"Open the damned vault," the robber said. "Open it or I'll blow off her purty li'l head."

Slocum saw how the tension was increasing fast. The other five robbers were getting antsy. They had cleaned out the cash drawers and were standing around getting more and more nervous because of their inexperience. Mention of the county sheriff put them even more on edge. The way their boss threatened the woman told Slocum he was sitting on a powder keg ready to explode.

People would die, most likely the lovely woman first, and then the rest of the people in the bank as the robbers panicked and lead began flying.

Slocum stepped forward, lowered his shoulder, and rammed hard into one of the men waggling a shotgun about. As he knocked the robber off balance, he went for his trusty Colt Navy. He got it out and fired at another robber. The .36-caliber slug barely grazed the man, but Slocum was so close the ignited powder set fire to his shirt, causing the others to stare at him.

This was all the opening Slocum needed. He dropped to one knee and sighted in on the robber threatening the woman. His slug went wide when the robber he had knocked down struggled to get up and his shotgun discharged accidentally. The man blew a two-foot-diameter hole in the floor and sent splinters flying in all directions. A long sharp one caught Slocum on the cheek. He fired just as he flinched, causing him to miss the ringleader.

"Kill them, kill them all!" shrieked the leader, but he was talking to empty air. The other five had hightailed it with their loot.

Seeing he had lost the upper hand, the robber grabbed the woman and dragged her across the lobby, using her as a shield to keep Slocum from blowing off his foul head. The woman showed good sense when she realized what was going on. She simply went limp and fell bonelessly from the man's grip.

Slocum fired. The robber returned fire, then ducked out the double doors. Already there came the thunder of hooves as the first of the robbers to run from the bank got their horses spurred into a full gallop.

Ignoring the blood trickling down his cheek, Slocum vaulted over the woman and ran to the front doors. He ducked back when a shotgun cut loose. Immediately behind it came a hail of bullets.

"Damnation," he said, recognizing the report of one of those six-shooters. Ignoring the danger, he plunged out into the burning midday Arizona sun and emptied his Colt at the retreating robbers. Slocum turned and saw Clay Tolliver sitting on the ground at the corner of the bank. His back was pressed against the crumbling adobe, and his gun slid from nerveless fingers.

"Clay!"

"Slocum, we done chased them varmints off. How'd that happen?"

Slocum shook his head. They had been casing the bank and had stopped a robbery instead. He had a minor wound, but from the look of the blood soaking Tolliver's shirt, the cowboy was in serious condition.

"Are you gents all right?" asked the banker, bustling out with a pearl-handled derringer in his hand, as if this would matter to the outlaws.

"He needs a doctor. Bad. My partner got off a couple shots at the robbers, but they got him in the chest," Slocum said.

"Grace, see if that good-for-nothing Doc Martin is sober enough to tend to this man."

Slocum saw the beautiful woman nod once, then lift her skirts and hurry off in search of the town sawbones.

"I hope you gents got enough money to pay for Doc Martin. He charges an arm and a leg for his services," the banker said.

Tolliver was past hearing. He had slumped over, still alive, but barely. Slocum stared at the banker.

"We kept your bank from getting robbed."

"And I, Seamus Reilly, want to be the first to thank you for being so civic-minded." He thrust out his hand.

"You're not offering to pay for my friend's doctoring?"

"I should say not. This is a dangerous country, and we all share equally in the risk of road agents and other social detritus. No reason this idea should not extend to all our burdens, be they financial or otherwise."

Pretty daughter or not, Reilly irked Slocum something fierce. Robbing the bank—and the arrogant Seamus Reilly—seemed more like something Slocum wanted to do now than when he had first walked in.

He put his arm around Tolliver's shoulders to support the man until the doctor and three liquored-up drunks from a nearby saloon came over to get his injured partner to the surgery.

Slocum glared at Seamus Reilly, who seemed oblivious

to everything around him. Slocum did not stop when Grace Reilly tried to speak to him. He had more important things to do, like seeing that his partner was properly tended to.

2

"Your friend's mighty lucky," said one of the drunks who had helped Slocum get Tolliver to the surgery. "Doc Martin's not dead-on-his-ass drunk yet. Don't think so, at least." The man hiccuped, as if showing exactly how far gone the town doctor might have been by a little past three in the afternoon.

Slocum laid Tolliver on an operating table and looked around the small surgery. He had seen worse, especially during the war when arms and legs got stacked like cordwood outside the medic's tent. This room smelled of carbolic acid, showing that the sawbones took time to clean up once and a while.

"Slocum," Tolliver said weakly. "We got them varmints, didn't we?"

"Don't talk. I'll see they get what's coming to them." Remembering how the banker had acted, Slocum added another name to the roster of men deserving of some frontier justice. Intentional or not, he and Tolliver had kept the bank from being robbed by a band of nervous thieves led by a cold-blooded killer.

They had shot down his partner. They would pay for it. Dearly.

"Where's the doctor?" Slocum said sharply. He looked around. The talkative drunk collapsed into a chair, his legs not strong enough to propel him in search of Martin.

"He'll be here soon, sir," said a worried voice. Grace Reilly bustled in, her long skirts rustling like a gentle wind in tall mountain ponderosa pines. "I would also like to apologize for my father. At times he can be overly brusque. The robbery disturbed him and he forgot his manners."

"I didn't want a reward," Slocum said, though that would have been helpful—and would have prevented Slocum from robbing the bank later. "The least he could do is pay for my friend's care."

"I'll see to the bill," Grace said. She averted her emerald eyes, and Slocum thought she blushed. He wondered what thoughts went through her mind to cause such a reaction. "I surely do appreciate what you did, you and your friend here. He reminds me so much of . . ." The lovely woman's words trailed off as she lost herself in some memory she did not share with Slocum.

She picked up Tolliver's limp hand and held it gently, stroking over the weathered top with her own softer fingers. Almost guiltily, she dropped it when Dr. Martin came in, grumbling to himself and crashing around like a bull in a china shop.

"Can't a body get a moment's peace? What the hell happened to this varmint? A shooting in the middle of the day? Again? Damn bastards don't even wait for the sun to go down no more." He roughly pushed Grace out of the way, dumped his black bag on the table beside Tolliver, and immediately began poking and prodding.

Slocum saw Tolliver flinch. His partner wasn't dead—yet. But from the blunt treatment he got at the doctor's hands, that condition might not last long.

"Can you patch him up, Doc?" Slocum asked.

"How the hell should I know? Get your butt outta here

and let a man work. You, too, missy. You get on back to the bank and tell that worthless father of yours he'd better not get sick or he'll pay the piper!"

Slocum took Grace by the elbow and steered her from the room before she could retort.

Outside in the hot sun, the dust rising all around as a fitful wind kicked down Neutral's main street, Slocum said to the banker's daughter, "You don't have to pay out of your own pocket. I'll see to my partner's care."

"What's his name?" she asked.

"Tolliver. Clay Tolliver. I'm John Slocum."

"Pleased to meet you, Mr. Slocum. Well, not *pleased*, not like this, but you know what I mean."

"From what the doc said, not many folks in Neutral care a whit for your pa."

"You can see why. He is downright ruthless when it comes to money and his darned old bank." Her lips thinned to a line. Slocum thought that made her look even prettier. Grace was a determined, spirited young lady.

"You have any ideas who it might have been holding up the bank?"

"Their names? Of course not. There have been all kinds of robberies these past few weeks. Increased traffic along the Gila Road by the Butterfield Company has something to do with it. And there is a new army post a couple dozen miles off."

"Your pa's bank handle the payroll?"

"He's trying. There is a bank in the town nearest Fort Carleton, but it lacks a decent vault. They use little more than a tin cash box to hold their depositors' money. We can—"

"That's all right," Slocum said, holding up his hand to stop the sales pitch. "I get the picture."

"Sorry. Some of my father's aggressiveness has worn off on me."

"Don't see it," Slocum said, smiling at her. That such

a lovely woman could end up in a miserable Arizona town like this was a cruel twist of fate, in Slocum's estimation.

"I really must return to the bank or Father will be furious."

"Reckon it doesn't take much for that to happen," Slocum observed.

"Thank you for understanding. And I *will* see that Clay—Mr. Tolliver—gets only the finest care. Dr. Martin seems a crusty old curmudgeon, but he is a good physician."

Slocum watched Grace hurry down the street, going back to the bank her father ran with an iron hand. Getting revenge on the robbers for gunning down Tolliver was high on Slocum's list of needful things, but right now he wanted to get out of the burning summer sun. He headed for the nearest saloon, then knew it wouldn't do him any good going in. Even if beer went for a nickel, he couldn't afford it.

He thrust his head into the water barrel at the side of the saloon, then cupped his hands and drank his fill. Something warned him, a sixth sense. He bent forward again, as if to drink more, but his hand went toward the ebony handle of his Colt Navy.

He turned slightly and looked behind him. On the covered walk stood a sturdily built man of average height staring at him. Slocum had seen him before, prior to the robbery. This was the man who had come out of the bank. The man reached up and twirled the tip of his mustache. The movement caused his coat to catch the wind blowing restlessly. Sunlight glinted off a bright star.

The law. Slocum wondered if he ought to draw and shoot it out or wait a spell. The lawman might be suspicious because of the robbery and nothing more, but Slocum carried a powerful lot of weight on his shoulders. Besides killing the judge, he had done a bit of cattle rustling and train robbing. For all he knew, the sheriff might have on his desk a stack of different wanted posters, all with Slocum's likeness on them.

Slocum half turned, his six-shooter coming out of his cross-draw holster, but the sheriff had vanished like dust in the wind. Feeling a mite foolish at such disquiet on his own part, Slocum shoved the six-gun back into its holster and washed his face off again. The hot wind cooled him and let him think better. What he needed more than anything else was some victuals. Victuals and a shot or two of whiskey. And even a few hours of sleep.

"You!" bellowed Dr. Martin, waddling up the street from the direction of his surgery. "Get your creaking bones into the saloon so I can tell you what's what."

Dr. Martin did not wait to see if Slocum obeyed. Slocum trailed him into the Dead Lizard Dance Hall. The doctor had already dropped into a rickety chair at what looked like his regular table. Slocum sat across from the man.

"Drink up, son, you'll need it for what I got to tell you," Dr. Martin said, indicating a quarter of a bottle of rye whiskey in the center of the table. Slocum poured a couple of fingers into a shot glass and knocked it back. It went down smooth and sat hard in his belly. He needed food as much as he did liquor right now.

"Tolliver die?" Slocum asked.

"Die? I don't let my patients die! Course not. Don't even whisper that or folks'll think I ain't no good as a sawbones. No, the varmint's alive and I intend to keep him that way, but it's gonna be a long, hard road for him. Damn hard."

Slocum had seen how the bullet had gone into Tolliver's chest on the lower left side. A wound there might have punctured a lung or gone through his heart. Since he was still alive, Slocum doubted Tolliver had been shot in the heart.

"Tricky work gettin' the lead out of him, yes, sir, damn

tricky," Dr. Martin said, working on his second drink to Slocum's one. "But you can't find a better doctor in these parts."

"How long?"

"How long's he got to live? Not long at all, if he keeps jumpin' in front of bank robbers with guns," Dr. Martin said.

"How long will he be laid up?"

The doctor shrugged. "Can't rightly say, but it'll be a couple of weeks. Lost a gallon of blood or two. And the bullet damaged his lung. Didn't exactly puncture it but came close, damn close. Creased it, left a nasty gouge. Bullet ran along the inside of a rib then and busted him up some inside. I sewed him up best I could so there's no more bleeding. Now we wait and see if he pulls through."

"If?"

"He will, damn your eyes," Dr. Martin said. The sawbones glared at Slocum. "Don't go criticizin' my work."

Slocum caught a reflection in the glass whiskey bottle, and turned in time to see the sheriff duck back out the wide-open front doors.

"Who's that?" he asked Martin.

"Sheriff Hardeen," the doctor answered. "Useless as tits on a bull, I'd say. Can't keep the peace in town and doesn't even serve process well. But the fools keep re-electing him 'cuz he don't ask for much in the way of salary."

"He seems mighty interested in me," Slocum said. "Why doesn't he just come over and say his piece?"

"You're a mighty threatening gent, that's why. Hardeen ain't the kind to rock the boat by actually doin' his job."

"Who's watching Tolliver?"

Dr. Martin turned sly. "The one what's paying for his care, that's who. I think Miss Reilly's feeling guilty about it and wants to put things right."

"Grace is with my partner?"

"Watching over him like some sweet angel of gracious mercy," Martin said, downing another drink. He'd had four in the span of Slocum's two, and didn't show the least bit of wooziness. The potent rotgut had already gone to Slocum's head and made him wobbly. He needed food more than he did any more liquor right now.

"Go on over to the bar and help yourself to a sandwich," Dr. Martin said. "Tell that idiot barkeep to put it on my bill." He laughed and added, "At least lunch is free here, even if it's danged near sundown." With that Martin got to his feet and made his way out of the Dead Lizard. For the first time, Slocum saw the unsteadiness in the doctor's gait.

As Dr. Martin left, he pushed past Sheriff Hardeen outside the saloon, who quickly vanished rather than spy on Slocum further. Frowning, Slocum turned to the barkeep and saw a plate of food had been shoved in front of him. He ate hungrily, not even bothering to thank the mousy man working as bartender.

As he ate, he thought hard. He could not leave Neutral until Tolliver was able to ride. From what Dr. Martin said, that might be two or three weeks. Slocum didn't cotton much to having the sheriff dog his steps every inch of the trail, but he figured Hardeen would get tired of it eventually and move on to other pursuits.

Pursuits.

The word burned in Slocum's mind until an idea formed and a slow smile came to his lips.

He must have looked feral, because the barkeep backed off and made a big point of talking to a burly miner at the far end of the bar. Slocum hardly noticed. He had a notion his time in Neutral might not be wasted, not if what Grace Reilly said was true about the robberies increasing.

"Water," Slocum called to the barkeep.

A short, dapper, clean-shaven man strutted into the sa-

loon and put his elbows down a couple feet from Slocum.
He eyed Slocum from foot to dusty hat, and then fixed a
steady gaze on his green eyes.

"That's no fit drink for a man, even in this parched
desert. Give him a shot of whiskey."

"Not the swill you give Dr. Martin," Slocum declared
to the barkeep. He had the uneasy feeling he had seen this
man before, but could not place him. He was too well
dressed to be one of the bank robbers—and he was too
short. Slocum would have noticed a man who hardly came
up to his chin.

"Much obliged," Slocum told him. "I've had quite a
day."

"You look down on your luck," the man said in a
friendly fashion, but the eyes were colder by the minute.
"You looking for action?"

"No money," Slocum said, accepting the whiskey, "so
you'd have to take an IOU if we got into a poker game."

"I wasn't talking about poker," the man said.

Slocum shook his head. "Prospects for a job in Neutral
don't look too good."

"A man with a gun can make his own prospects."

Slocum turned wary. Sheriff Hardeen had spied on him
and then turned and run. This sawed-off gent didn't sport
a lawman's badge on his fancy duds, but with Hardeen
looking over his shoulder all the time, Slocum wasn't going to throw in with anyone who might ride on the wrong
side of the law.

Besides, Slocum had a plan. A good one.

"Reckon that's true, if a man has a mind to. I don't.
What I want is for a friend to get back into condition to
ride, and then all Neutral will see of us is a dust cloud."

The man tipped his head, as if saying, "Too bad," and
then got down to some serious drinking without saying
any more to Slocum. Slocum finished his whiskey,
thanked the man, then left the Dead Lizard in search of

somewhere to sleep for the night. His heart beat a little faster when he noticed Grace Reilly leaving Dr. Martin's surgery. She must have been keeping watch over Clay Tolliver.

"Lucky devil," Slocum said, then went to negotiate with the livery stable owner for an expanse of hay to unroll his blanket on.

3

"Two holdups in the last month?" Slocum asked, shaking his head as he commiserated with the stagecoach agent. The man's filthy, tangled beard sported a small black bug crawling in and out of the greasy strands, forcing Slocum to concentrate on the man's words rather than watching the slow insect progress upward to the chin.

"Can't stop 'em. Sheriff Hardeen's doin' what he can, but he can't be everywhere all the time."

"You're about the first agent to excuse the local law for not putting an end to the robberies," Slocum said. "The bank was held up yesterday. Does it get hit like your stagecoaches?"

The station agent shook his head, scratched himself, and took a swig out of a canteen. Slocum was sure it held something other than water from the strong odor.

"Bank's got a lot of guards, or it did. Them robbers are startin' to shoot the guards, and that makes most folks a bit skittish to take such a jackass job."

"I can understand why," Slocum said. "You think it's one gang or several doing all the dirty work?"

He glanced over his shoulder. Sheriff Hardeen stood in the shadows of a hardware store, watching him like a hawk. When Hardeen saw he had been detected, he slipped down an alley and vanished. Slocum waited a moment before turning back to the Butterfield agent. Three men rode together out of town, looking intent. One was the short, dapper man he had run into the day before. Now the man wore a clean duster and looked for all the world as if he was going courting, all gussied up, bathed, and shaved. The two men with him were scruffier-looking, but cleaner than the run-of-the-mill resident of Neutral.

"You know those gents?" Slocum asked, indicating the small man and his two henchmen.

"Never seen 'em before. Neutral's a strange hole in the ground," the agent said, scratching hard at a nit. "We got lots of fellas ridin' through all the time. Some look for silver and gold up there in the mountains. A few find it. Neutral used to be a rip-roarin' boomtown, but no more. The gold mine're peterin' out. But the Gila Trail's runnin' full tilt now, a half dozen stages a week comin' 'n goin'."

"All loaded with gold?" asked Slocum.

The agent squinted at him, spat, and then said, "Can't say."

"Sorry, didn't mean for it to sound the way it did," Slocum said, realizing the man thought he was being pumped for information that could be used by a road agent. "I need a job real bad. My partner's laid up over at Dr. Martin's, and I thought I might get a job riding shotgun messenger."

"Ain't got anything right now." The agent laughed, and it sounded almost evil. "You might try at Reilly's bank. *He* can always use a new guard or two. But then he don't pay squat, and they get shot up somethin' fierce."

"Thanks," Slocum said, having learned what he needed to know.

He ambled off, aware Hardeen was again dogging his steps. Slocum wanted to tell him the short, well-dressed man was likely more a threat to the peace of the county, but he held his tongue. Hardeen had yet to approach him and say howdy.

Slocum checked the ammo in his Colt Navy and then mounted his horse. He rode down the back streets and out of Neutral, heading into the hills. The Gila Trail was well marked. He and Tolliver had come along it from the west, and had seen several places where a clever band of highwaymen might waylay a stagecoach. Slocum pulled down the brim of his hat to shade his eyes and set off, letting his horse set its own gait in the growing desert heat.

Less than an hour out of Neutral, Slocum halted on a rise and smiled. In the distance rattled and clanked a Concord coach, heading toward town. In the precise spot he had considered for a robbery huddled a half dozen highwaymen.

Robbers.

Slocum drew the Winchester from its sheath and made sure the magazine was full. He checked his Colt Navy again, then rearranged the contents of his saddlebags so his spare loaded cylinders were handy. He wasn't going head-to-head with the road agents, but if he robbed them as he planned, he might find himself in a world of trouble fast.

Slocum went over his plan and liked it more as he watched. The highwaymen took the risk of stealing the lock box from the stagecoach. Whatever they got would be divided up later. Slocum intended to steal their booty before then. Rob the robbers. It felt good to him. Who were they going to complain to?

He urged his horse down the sandy slope and circled, going away from the road where he thought the robbers would run. Slocum pictured the robbery perfectly in his head. The ripple of echoes from gunshots came about when he thought. He reined back and waited. The robbers ought to be making their getaway soon, down the dry wash to the west of where he rode.

The sounds reaching him ten minutes later confirmed his suspicion. The robbers laughed and joked, their voices carrying on the dry desert air. Of their horses Slocum heard nothing. That didn't matter. He knew where the men rode, and would keep pace with them until they pitched their camp.

Then he would rob them.

He might get enough to pay Dr. Martin and maybe buy a decent meal for himself. His belly rubbed up against his backbone. The sandwich right after Tolliver got shot was all Slocum had eaten since reaching Neutral.

An hour riding made Slocum anxious to get the thieving from thieves over and done with. He boldly rode up a sandy rise and studied the terrain. To his surprise, the highwaymen had already camped, and he had passed them by. He had expected them to ride into the mountains and camp there, well away from any pursuit by the law.

But then, the law didn't seem too inclined to leave Neutral.

Slocum started to backtrack when he got an uneasy feeling. The hair on the back of his neck rose, as if someone had sighted in on him. During the war he had been a sniper, and had always wondered if his targets knew they were doomed before he squeezed off the killing rounds. Slocum jerked around to check his backtrail.

He went cold inside when he saw a half dozen riders coming toward him.

He reached for his rifle, then stopped when he saw Sheriff Hardeen at the front of the posse.

"Don't go doing anything dumb, Slocum," the sheriff called out.

"I'm on the track of some stagecoach robbers," Slocum explained. "They're—"

"Right over the hill. We know," Hardeen said coldly. "You're messin' where you don't belong, Slocum."

"Who are they?" Slocum asked, indicating the men

with the sheriff. "Didn't know you had this many deputies."

"They're all legal," Hardeen said defensively. "A vigilance committee from town."

"We call ourselves the Gila Rangers," said a man riding at the sheriff's shoulder. "We're gonna keep the peace in this county, come Hell or high water." The man looked more in charge than the sheriff. He had a hard look lacking in Hardeen, and his pistol was slung in a cross-draw holster like Slocum's. The butt of the six-shooter had seen considerable wear too. Slocum did not doubt the rest of the six-gun had been well used as well. This one, unlike the sheriff, was a man used to living hard.

"Might be I can join up," Slocum said. "I want some revenge on the owlhoots who shot my partner. Reckon it might be them what robbed the coach."

"We'll handle it," the man with Hardeen said. "The sheriff told you to hightail it. I'd do as he says."

The alternative hung between them. Slocum wasn't anxious to shoot it out with the man—or his cronies.

"Not likely to see high water, not in this heat," Slocum said.

"Get on back to town, Slocum, and let us enforce the law."

Slocum considered asking about a reward for tracking the robbers, then decided against it. Sheriff Hardeen was not in charge of this posse, no matter what he said. The hard-looking gunman with him called the shots, and he wasn't the sort who shared anything, much less a reward.

Slocum wondered if they had the same idea he had. Track the highwaymen, rob them, then bring in the dead bodies for any reward Butterfield might post.

"Whatever you say, Sheriff," Slocum said, turning his horse back toward Neutral. It galled him to ride away like this, but he saw nothing to be gained in fighting the vigilantes.

The Gila Rangers they had called themselves.

For two cents, Slocum would have buried the lot of them in the dry bed of the Gila River.

He got back to Neutral a little after sundown. The desert cooled fast and cold wind cut at his face now. The change from the burning heat was welcome, however. Slocum wished he had money enough to get some chow. He traded some small chores for the stable owner feeding his and Tolliver's horses and keeping them curried, but Slocum was on his own.

He left the horse at the stable and started for Doc Martin's surgery to see how Tolliver was getting along. Worrying about his own hunger could wait.

He slipped into the darkened room and went to Tolliver's side. The man was pale but slept easily. His breathing sounded regular, and he did not appear to be in pain. That was all Slocum could hope for. He turned to leave and found the doorway blocked.

"I wanted to check on him too," Grace Reilly said.

"Thanks," Slocum said. "I'm sure Clay would appreciate it."

"Is he all right?"

"Seems right as rain," Slocum said. "Or he will be," he said.

Slocum left, closing the door after him. Grace remained at his side.

"Anything I can do for you, Miss Reilly?"

"Please, call me Grace. We got off on such a bad foot."

"I wouldn't say that. Looks like it was your pa's doing that caused bad feelings."

"I'm paying Dr. Martin for his services." She turned a little bitter. "He's drinking up the fee over at the Dead Lizard."

"Life can be hard for a man like him," Slocum said. "He's got some book learning. Other than you, who else in Neutral has ever read a book?"

"There might be quite a few. You don't know. And why do you think I am educated?"

He laughed. "I'd be a fool if I didn't hear the book learning in your words. Boston?"

"You are very good, Mr. Slocum."

"John," he said. They walked together down the street, their hips brushing. He felt warmer with every step, and it wasn't from the desert. If anything, the wind blowing restlessly now was downright cold. All the heat came from within—and was caused by Grace.

"Where are you staying? John." She looked up at him, her pale face the loveliest vision he had ever seen, including some mighty fine mirages out in the desert.

"In the stable. Both Tolliver and I are tapped out."

"Tolliver," she said. "Clay Tolliver. Tell me about him."

"He's my partner," Slocum said. "That's about all I ever needed to know."

"You trust him, though?"

"Of course. Why are you asking?"

"The pair of you, both so brave and—" Grace moved even closer. Slocum felt the pressure of her body warmly against his. She tipped her face up to his, her eyes hooded and lips slightly parted. He hardly knew what was going on, but with such a blatant invitation he was not going to turn her down.

He kissed Grace on her red, full lips.

Then she kissed him back with more passion than he had thought could be locked in her trim, proper body.

They clung to each other, tongues exploring as their kisses deepened. Slocum broke off as he kissed along the line of her jaw and captured the nub of her earlobe. He nibbled gently on it. She melted in his arms as if she had turned to wax in the bright noonday sun. Turning slightly away from him, the woman clung fervently to him. He kissed the nape of her neck and felt her begin to tremble.

"There's a special place I know. Rattlesnake Springs, off the Gila Road up in the foothills. It is so quiet and romantic. Shady, and oh, oh!" She gasped as he sucked at her earlobe. Slocum felt the redhead begin to sag. He held her in his strong arms. She pressed even harder against him.

"The stable," she said. "We can go to the stable. I don't want to wait until we can get out of town and go all the way to Rattlesnake Springs."

"Are you sure?" he asked, startled at his good fortune.

"Yes!"

She almost dragged him after her into the stable with its fragrant straw and other heady, earthy odors. Barely had the door slammed behind Slocum than Grace spun about and threw her arms around his neck.

He had thought her earlier kisses were potent. These were stronger than any whiskey. He got a little light-headed. Somehow they sank down into an empty stall and lay full length in the clean straw. Slocum kept kissing as Grace's hands started to roam, to seek intimate spots, to free parts of his anatomy.

"So big," she sighed, stroking up and down his length with her fingers curled seductively around him. "And so wasted. I want it where it'll do more good."

"Where's that?" he asked, working on the buttons on her blouse. He pushed aside her frilly undergarments and revealed the twin globes of her ample breasts. They were firm, capped with coppery nubs. He gobbled them like a starved man. He licked and sucked and caused Grace to arch her back in an attempt to cram those succulent breasts fully into his mouth.

"So good, John, so nice." She wiggled and shoved out her chest to be sure his mouth worked on every square inch of her tender flesh.

"Umm," was all he could say. He loved the taste of her

body almost as much as he did the pressure of her fingers circling his manhood.

Slocum pushed her blouse away and exposed the slight dome of her belly. He kissed as he went lower, only to be thwarted by the complicated tangle of her skirt and undergarments.

"Let me," she said. Grace released him for a moment, but it was worth it. For both of them.

She hiked her skirts and exposed paradise to Slocum's lusting gaze. Between her milky thighs nestled a rusty-fleeced triangle. He thrust his finger into the middle, sinking knuckles deep into her interior. Again she gasped and arched her back. Her rump rose off the straw as she ground her groin into his hand.

"I want to give you more 'n that," Slocum said, pulling his damp fingers from her most intimate recess.

"Yes, yes, now, John, now, do it now!"

She grabbed frantically at him and pulled him down on top of her. The woman's legs spread wantonly for him as he sank balls-deep into her. Grace moaned and thrashed around, impaled on his meaty spike. Slocum was lost in a different world now, one of intense pleasure.

He felt as if a warm velvet glove enfolded him now. When Grace began tensing and relaxing, he felt the warmth in his balls change. It felt as if she had lit a fuse to a powder keg.

Slocum began moving, slowly at first, then building speed and depth of penetration. Every stroke caused Grace to lift off the straw. She reached down and grabbed at her knees to hold them up and wide, affording Slocum the best possible entry.

He did not disappoint her. The carnal friction built and flooded through her until she cried out in sexual release. Slocum gasped as it felt like a mine shaft collapsing all around him. He had thought her fingers were firm around him. Now she threatened to crush him flat with her strong inner muscles.

Slocum thrust even faster, even harder. His hips took over and desire burned at his brain. The fire that had ignited deep in him began to spread, to burn along his length. Slocum fought to hold it back as long as possible.

He was distantly aware of Grace crying out in joy once again. Then he became locked in his own ultimate pleasure.

Spent, he lay beside her and stared into her half-closed green eyes. They were lost in a muzzy afterglow Slocum wished could last forever. In some ways holding the beautiful woman after such an intense lovemaking was as good as he could expect from life.

"What are you thinking, John?"

"This is better than any reward your pa might have offered," he said.

"Well, I hope so! I—"

Slocum silenced her with a kiss. And then they started all over again, going slower this time, making it last and delivering even more enjoyment.

4

"I would, John, I really would. If I could," Grace Reilly said. She looked apprehensively over her shoulder in the direction of the bank, as if expecting her father to come boiling out. Slocum had hung around Neutral for a couple days now, and saw how things worked. Seamus Reilly called the shots in town, at least among the law-abiding citizens owning businesses. No doubt he owned their mortgages, and probably the inventories in their stores.

That Grace feared her father bothered him, but Slocum was more annoyed that he could not get a job as bank guard. He and Grace had enjoyed each other's company every night, or at least when she was not taking care of Clay Tolliver. She spent more time with the wounded man than his partner.

Slocum shrugged that off. He had another ax to grind. He needed money, and his scheme of robbing the road agents working along the Gila Road and stealing anything they took from the Butterfield Stage had not panned out. Sheriff Hardeen had been like a second shadow ever since their meeting out on the trail of the outlaws. Slocum couldn't help noticing that Hardeen and the self-styled Gila Rangers had not returned to Neutral with either the

33

Butterfield strongbox or any prisoners. Vigilante commit-
tees tended to string up the objects of their attention, but
they also bragged on it afterward.

There had been a stony silence about the Gila Rangers
and their activity. A strange silence, as if everyone in
Neutral was afraid of even mentioning them.

For all that, the town was quiet enough. It was hard to
believe the storm of robbery swirled around as it did.

"John, I'll try to find you a job. It won't be much, but
there are a few people in town who owe me favors."

"Don't worry about it, Grace," he told the lovely redhead. "I'll find something. You're being too good to Tolliver and me as is."

"I do wish Father would be more reasonable."

"He says he's not in business to win friends," Slocum
pointed out, "and he's succeeding. Haven't heard anyone
in town say a good word about him."

She looked fearful, then smiled. It made her look more
like a death's skull than a beautiful woman. A chill went
down Slocum's spine to see Grace with such an expression.

"He's a cruel, mean man, John. I know it. I've lived
with it all my life and hate him for it. But he *is* my father,
and I owe him."

Slocum knew how it was. Blood was thicker than water, but if he saw Seamus Reilly raise his hand to his
daughter, there'd be a dead banker in Neutral. Slocum
wondered if anyone, including Sheriff Hardeen and his
Gila Rangers, would even notice.

"I'll buy you lunch, John. Please. It's the least I can
do."

"I've already seen what's the most you can do," he said,
grinning.

"Have you now, Mr. Slocum?" She beamed. Her beauty
was breathtaking. "Perhaps I've been holding back."

"If you have, I might be laid up alongside Tolliver if

you ever uncork. There's only so much a body can take."

They went to a small cafe down the street. As they ate, Slocum noticed the increased activity throughout Neutral. The Gila Rangers started at one end of town and swept along the main street, questioning people, wrangling with men they considered to be loitering, and generally stirring people up.

"I wish the sheriff would get rid of them," Grace said, looking apprehensive. "They frighten me."

"Can't say I'm too happy with them either. Why does Hardeen allow them free rein?"

Grace shrugged. "He is not a strong man. The vigilante who is always with him—Walker is all I've ever heard him called—seems more in charge than the sheriff."

"If Hardeen needed deputies, why didn't he pin stars on their chests and make them official?" Slocum ate slowly, watching as the man Grace had named, the same man he had seen calling the shots with Hardeen, pushed and shoved his way down the street until men turned tail and dived for their burrows like frightened rabbits. "For all that, why haven't Walker and the vigilantes cut down on crime?"

"I hadn't thought about that," Grace said, frowning. "Perhaps there hasn't been time. I never noticed Walker and the others until after the stagecoach got held up for the third time."

"Any of Walker's vigilantes look like the men who held up your pa's bank?"

"You think the Gila Rangers are outlaws?" Grace laughed and shook her head. "Hardeen might be weak, but I don't think he is a crook."

"Pay's lousy," Slocum pointed out.

"He makes more as sheriff than he ever did breaking his back up in the mountains working a gold claim. Doubt he took more than a few ounces out of that mine of his."

"So becoming sheriff was a move up in the world?"

That didn't surprise Slocum. He finished his meal, shoved back the plate, and considered asking for more. But Grace was paying, and he hated taking charity from a woman. She was willing—in a lot of ways—but it rankled. A man provided, not the woman.

"You might say that," Grace said. She eyed him hungrily, and Slocum knew what she wanted was not food. But it was the middle of the day and he wanted to find someone, anyone, in Neutral willing to put him to work. The lack of money was starting to bother him.

"I'll see you later," he said, heading off her request. It must have been hell for a lovely woman like Grace in a frontier town like Neutral. He was surprised she hadn't fallen for some tinhorn gambler with slick ways and honeyed words. Or maybe she had, and was looking for someone with more substance. Slocum didn't want to dwell on the woman's reasons for taking up with him, since he could not offer her that much.

"I'll go see how Clay is doing," she said. "But I need to stop by the bank first. Walk me back, please, John."

"I can certainly do that, and with pleasure," he said. Slocum glanced out into the street, expecting to see a knot of Gila Rangers waiting to badger him. To his surprise, the vigilantes had vanished. The hot sun must finally have gotten to them.

Slocum and Grace walked down the dusty street toward the bank. Grace chattered away about this and that, but Slocum listened with half an ear. Something felt wrong to him. Worse than the gnawing sensation of something wrong, he could not focus in on what it might be. He looked around and saw nothing.

"Are you all right, John? You look distracted."

"Can't say. Let's get out of the sun. I swear, it'll cook your brains even with a hat on your head."

Grace laughed lightly, and went into the cool interior of the bank as Slocum held the door. They stepped in, and Slocum knew what it was that was bothering him.

To one side of the bank had been tethered five horses. He ought to have wondered why so many customers had come to the bank at the same time in the heat of the day. As he and Grace felt the cool created by the thick adobe walls close around them, he also saw the leveled six-guns of five masked robbers.

"They came back," Grace whispered.

Slocum knew better than to go for his six-shooter. One mistake and bullets would fly. Grace was directly in the line of fire, as was another customer, a grizzled miner whose work-bleary eyes were wide with fear. He saw death coming at him.

So did Slocum.

"Drop that fancy hogleg," came the shrill command. Slocum recognized the robber as one from the prior day—the bank robber who had panicked. From the way he spoke now, he was equally nervous and as likely to shoot as to run if anything went wrong.

"I'll drop my gunbelt," Slocum said.

"Do it real slow-like!"

"John," Grace said, and he wasn't able to figure out what she wanted from him. To defend her honor and save the bank again? Or was she telling him not to be a hero?

Slocum didn't have to be told how quickly he could become a dead hero. The robbers had the drop on him. The slightest mistake would cause them all to jerk back on five triggers. He unfastened his gunbelt and eased it to the dusty sawed-plank floor. As he straightened, Slocum waited for a slug to rip through his heart.

He did not relax when the robbers didn't plug him outright.

"This is the little lady we been waitin' for," said the robber Slocum pegged as leader. "Open that vault in the back. Open it or your friend here'll die!"

"Go on and shoot him now," Grace said hotly. "I don't

know the combination. Only my father does."

"That's right, mister," said a teller. "Mr. Reilly don't trust any of us, least of all his daughter."

Slocum would have laughed if death hadn't been so close. He believed Seamus Reilly trusted no one, including Grace.

The robber looked around, studying faces. All the employees nodded. The miner spat a gob of tobacco and missed the cuspidor by a foot. The brown gob spread on the floor, staining it permanently.

"What we gonna do?" asked the one with the shrill voice. "We don't have no dynamite to blow the damn thing!"

"Shut up," snapped the leader. "We'll wait for him. He'll be back from lunch to count his money. He's the type who doesn't trust anyone, right? Then he's not going to let a bunch of thieves like them run the bank on their own."

Slocum had to admit the leader had pegged Seamus Reilly well. But the situation grew increasingly tense as every minute passed.

Grace jumped when the front doors opened and her father came bustling in.

"What's wrong with you?" Seamus Reilly bellowed. "Get to work, to work, you slackers!"

The leader of the bank robbers stepped up and slugged Reilly behind the ear. The impact of the long pistol barrel with Reilly's head echoed like a gunshot. Reilly fell to his knees, looking up as if he had been betrayed.

"What's going on?"

"You ain't that stupid, banker," snapped the leader. "We're robbing your damn bank. This time we're doin' it right. Open the vault for us, and we'll be on our way."

"Go to Hell, sir!"

"Wait!" cried Grace, reaching out to stop the robber from pistol-whipping her father. "If you hurt him, you'll never get into the vault. He *is* the only one who knows the combination."

Slocum took Grace's arm and pulled her back, wishing she would shut up. Drawing attention to herself was a quick way to get planted out in the town cemetery. He deflected attention from the woman by stepping between her and the robber.

"The banker's going to do what you tell him. Aren't you, Reilly?" Slocum's voice was colder than a winter storm, and his green eyes were twin daggers stabbing deep into Seamus Reilly's soul, what there was left of it. The banker puffed up with indignation, and Slocum wanted to grab the six-shooter from the robber and buffalo the banker himself.

"No!"

"We can kill your daughter," the leader said, pointing his six-gun at Grace. This was what Slocum had wanted to avoid. He tensed, every muscle like a steel spring really to unwind. It would be bloody, but he wouldn't let the man gun down an innocent woman, no matter that her father had virtually demanded it.

"Or we can start killing your employees one by one." The robber fired, tearing a splinter off the counter in front of a teller. The man jumped and clutched at his belly, but the slug had not hit him.

"Naw, that don't move you none, does it?" The leader fired again. This time his slug ripped through Seamus Reilly's upper thigh. The banker let out a yelp like a stepped-on dog.

"You animal!"

"Make it easy on yourself. Open the vault." The leader fired again, this time his slug ripping out a chunk of Reilly's upper arm. The banker bled from two wounds now, both on his left side. "If I get down to my last bullet, I don't reckon I'll waste it on your arm or leg. I'll put it smack in your putrid head!"

He shoved the still-smoking six-shooter into Reilly's face.

For the first time, the banker's bravado faded and he blanched.

"I'll open it. T-to save my daughter and t-the others."

Slocum felt nothing but contempt for the man, but whatever his reason for caving in to the robbers' demands, it didn't matter as much as keeping people alive. Time for retribution would come later.

"John, can you do anything?"

Grace clutched his arm so tightly she cut off circulation. Slocum shook his head as he watched the robbers. There wasn't anything he could do to stop the robbery this time. Before, he had taken the robbers by surprise. Now they held the upper hand. Two swung sawed-off shotguns around like the heads of coiled rattlers, going this way and that, ready to spew leaden poison. Two others jumped and jerked about nervously as they followed Reilly and their leader to the back room where the tall black steel safe stood.

"Open it," ordered the robber.

"If you hadn't shot me, I'd be better equipped for the chore," Seamus Reilly said. The robber read the man aright. Reilly was summoning his courage again. And the robber did what Slocum would have in his place. He shot Seamus Reilly in the right leg.

"You fiend!"

"Open the vault," ordered the robber. "No more jawing."

Grace sucked in her breath as her father hesitated. She knew he considered resisting some more. Then he sagged and turned to the vault. With shaking fingers, he spun the big dial on the steel safe. It took three tries before the doors swung back, but swing back they did.

Slocum's eyes widened at the sight of stacks of greenbacks. Bags of coins on the lower shelves must have weighed twenty pounds each from the way the robbers stumbled off balance when they pulled them from the vault.

"We did it, we did it!" cried one robber.

"Get the hell out," Seamus Reilly said. "You've got everything of value in this bank. Get out."

Slocum had seen whipped men before. If they had cut off Reilly's balls, they could not have defeated him more. The man lived for what had been in that vault. Slocum felt a passing pity for him, an emotion quickly replaced when he saw the leader of the robbers lifting his six-gun.

Slocum slammed hard into Grace, knocking her to the side. They crashed together to the floor, with Slocum atop the struggling woman. She stained her blouse in the gob of tobacco the miner had spat earlier, but she was in a corner and out of the line of fire.

The report from the robber's pistol echoed in the adobe bank, the report from the shot that bored out Seamus Reilly's brains.

Laughing, the robbers took their booty and ran from the bank. Slocum held Grace down until he heard the thunder of hooves vanish in the distance.

They were safe—and he had to figure a way of breaking it gently to Grace Reilly that her father had been murdered.

5

Slocum pushed away from Grace Reilly and looked around the bank lobby. The room felt closed in and dangerous now. No one moved. No one spoke. The acrid stench of gunpowder hung heavy in the air. The tellers stared straight ahead, as if they could vanish if they didn't move a muscle. The old miner finally broke the silence by letting out a loud "Yippeeee!"

"What are you crowing about, old man?" snapped Slocum. He grabbed his six-shooter and strapped it on. All the while, he stared past the tellers into the back room where Seamus Reilly lay facedown on the floor. Blood from his head wound trickled out and through the floorboards into thirsty sand below. Slocum knew dead men didn't bleed, but there was no question about Reilly's condition.

Maybe his feet were higher than his head and the blood leaked out. Whatever the cause, his heart had stopped beating with the robber's last shot.

"Papa!" cried Grace. Slocum grabbed her and swung her about. He shoved her into the miner's arms.

"Hold her," he said.

"Thass 'bout the best thing what's happened to me today," the man said. Slocum glared at him, and the man subsided.

A quick check verified what Slocum instinctively knew. Seamus Reilly was dead, dead, dead.

"Get the sheriff," he called. Someone raced off. Slocum did not care who it was—until Grace dropped to her knees beside him. The miner had lit out to fetch the law.

"He's dead, isn't he? He gave them what they wanted, and they killed him. How could they?"

"Come on," Slocum said, gently pulling Grace away. He had not liked Seamus Reilly. He liked him even less dead for the agony he caused his daughter. "You have someone you can stay with?"

"Where are you going?" Grace looked panicked.

"After them. I don't think Sheriff Hardeen is likely to be too eager to find the robbers."

"No, John, they'll kill you too!"

"They can't go scot-free," Slocum said. "If they aren't brought to justice, they'll kill others."

"But, John!"

She clung to him. Hot, salty tears stained his shirt as he held Grace close. Then he pushed her away.

"Time's a'wasting," he told her. "I'm not going to get hurt. They'll be the ones who die. I promise."

"John," she said, sobbing. "Go, go on. Do what you have to."

He nodded, wondered fleetingly where she would find shelter from this emotional storm, then dashed for the stable. His horse complained about going out in the torrid noonday sun, but Slocum kept urging the horse into motion until the animal gave in. At first Slocum couldn't find the robbers' trail. No one in Neutral had noticed a band of masked men riding out hellbent for leather.

He had not expected more. A half mile outside of town to the west he found the outlaws' trail. It led into the foothills, so he picked up the pace until his horse balked.

He kept pushing the horse because he would lose the robbers if they reached rockier terrain. Trailing in the dust was hard. On rock it would be impossible.

But Slocum was determined.

The bright moonlight turned the land to liquid silver. Slocum knelt, scratched his head, and tried to make out the conflicting spoor he got. The robbers had ridden with a purpose, apparently knowing exactly where they were headed. That meant they had a hideout somewhere in the mountains west of Neutral. It also meant Slocum had to be careful not to blunder onto a sentry waiting to put a slug in anyone on his gang's trail.

The crossing and recrossing tracks of two groups kept Slocum guessing. Tracking in the mountains was a fool's errand most times, but the narrow canyons and the fact that the robbers didn't cover their trail at any point made it easier for him.

"Who is this? Did they even see each other?" He circled the sandy spit where the tracks had become muddled by the relentless wind blowing down the canyon, moving sand and kicking up dust into the air. During the day that wind had felt like staring into an open blast furnace. Now the air carried an icy knife edge to it.

And the tracks were all the more roiled as the wind fitfully swirled.

"Two groups, each about five men, and I think they did see each other. I think they talked a spell." His horse nickered in protest. It was tired and had no desire to stay on the trail all night.

Slocum ignored the equine protests and sorted out what he knew. The road agents might have a gang bigger than the handful that had robbed the bank and killed Seamus Reilly. It accounted for the many robberies if two bands of five or six ran wild across southern Arizona. And Slocum might have chanced on the two groups meeting here.

He swallowed hard at the thought he might be taking on ten men instead of five. With judicious sniping, he could come out on top of five. He had no chance to take ten, if they didn't cut and run, reducing the odds. If they had a decent leader to whip them into an attacking party, Slocum would find himself buzzard bait before dawn.

"Five, ten, a thousand," he said to himself. "It doesn't matter. Somebody's going to pay for murdering Reilly."

He walked slowly from the sandy spit, and found himself hiking up a steep rise, loose stones clattering under his feet. Slocum worried about the noise. If he had to pick a hideout, this would be the way to it. Several men—such as a posse—trying to sneak up on the camp would give themselves away pronto.

At the top of the rise he saw the tracks continued along the ridge, meandering in and out of clumps of ponderosa pines. The night turned colder, but Slocum warmed to the chase. He was close. He felt it in his bones.

The faint whiff of burning pinyon on the night wind convinced him he had found the robbers. He tethered his horse some distance downwind from the outlaw camp and advanced slowly, scouting out the opposition.

He hid behind a tall pine and peered around the thick trunk. A half dozen men passed around cans of beans. Two blackened pots were thrust into the fire to boil coffee. His sensitive nose didn't pick up any hint of the coffee; it wasn't brewed yet.

But six men? What had he missed? If the two groups had swapped men, that might explain why the robbers had an extra man now.

"Give me a good reason," said a cold voice. Slocum heard the six-shooter cocking, and knew he couldn't dodge fast enough. The other man had the drop on him— and Slocum didn't even know where the gunman was.

"Just wondering about getting some food," Slocum said. "I've been on the trail a spell and—"

"Slocum!"

Slocum spun, hand going for his Colt Navy. But he stopped when he found himself face-to-face with the Gila Ranger named Walker. The way Walker had him covered with the big Remington in his hand stopped Slocum dead in his tracks.

"Walker," he said. "Fine night to be out riding, isn't it?"

"What are you looking for? Trouble?"

"You might say that," Slocum answered. Walker hadn't cut him down on the spot. Slocum didn't know why, but it could only mean he had some breathing room. "I'm on the trail of the bank robbers. The ones who gunned down Seamus Reilly."

"Fancy that," Walker said. "So are we. This here's my gang of Gila Rangers." He motioned with his Remington. Slocum kept his hands out from his body, but didn't put them into the air. Somehow, this compromise suited them both. For the moment.

As they neared the fire, the Gila Rangers all went for their guns.

"What the hell's goin' on, Walker?" demanded one of the men.

"I went to take a leak and found Slocum here," Walker said. He motioned for Slocum to sit on a log across from him. Slocum caught the first scent of boiling coffee. It made his mouth water.

"Go on, have a cup." Walker tossed him a battered tin cup. Slocum poured himself some of the brew, noting how vile it was. He didn't care. It went down hot and the warmth stayed with him.

"Thanks."

"You tracked the varmints all the way from Neutral?" asked Walker. He motioned to the others to keep their tater traps shut.

"All the way. Reckon I got confused. Two groups, each

about five riders, crossed a few miles back. I must have gotten on your trail by accident."

"You're a mighty fine trailsman, Slocum."

Slocum said nothing. Walker put his six-shooter away in his cross-draw holster, but Slocum knew trying to shoot his way out of the Gila Rangers' camp would be folly. Slocum could never get more than two or three of them before the rest filled him with slugs.

"We can use a man like you in our posse."

"I work alone," Slocum said. The bitter coffee cut at his tongue now as if he had drunk razors. It was still better than nothing.

"Hand him a can of beans, Tex." A man built like a mountain tossed Slocum an unopened can of beans. Slocum hastily used his knife to cut through the lid, and began scooping out the contents. He had been too eager to bring to justice the men who had killed the banker to stop and hunt for food.

"You look like you could use three squares a day, Slocum," said Walker.

"Not bad, when I can get them."

"Throw in with us. You track like an Injun, and we need that. Especially in these hills. Never saw so damned much rock in all my born days. We can use you, and you'll get regular meals and maybe a buck or two along the way."

"Sheriff Hardeen pay you?"

"No more than any other citizen of Neutral," said Walker, avoiding a direct answer of Slocum's question. "We do a service, we get paid for it. Simple as that."

Another man would have thought Walker meant the people of Neutral all chipped in and paid for this informal posse. Where the Gila Rangers really got their money was from somewhere else. Slocum might have confused the two groups of riders, but he didn't think so. He had tracked the bank robbers.

And ended up in the Gila Rangers' camp.

"Why you askin' *him* to join?" whined a man on the far side of the campfire. The shrill voice was familiar enough that Slocum thought he recognized it. This gent had held a scattergun on him and Grace earlier in the day—during the robbery.

"He's got what we need. I can tell from the look of that hunk of iron you carry that you can use it. That so, Slocum?"

Slocum wasn't the bragging kind. He pulled more beans from the airtight and only shrugged. Eating their chow wasn't going to change him any. Except to make him ornerier when it came to bringing them to justice.

"We're on their trail too. We picked it up back a ways. Want to ride with us while we find them varmints?"

"How far ahead of you are they?"

"Not too far. We figure they've bedded down for the night. We ride in a few minutes, we overtake them, and then . . ." Walker's voice trailed off, leaving the results to Slocum's imagination.

"Any reward for them?"

"Not that we know, but the bank might be inclined to pony up a few hundred for us. Not every day its owner gets cut down like that." A note of excitement came to Walker's voice, as if he was reliving pulling the trigger and watching Seamus Reilly die. Or was this only Slocum's imagination? As much as he hated to admit it, he had no proof the Gila Rangers had robbed the Neutral bank.

"I'll ride with you for a spell," Slocum said, belching. He washed down the beans with more bad coffee. "When we going after them?" He thought Walker was lying about being on the robbers' trail and wanted to call his bluff.

"Tex, you and the others ready? Then let's ride."

Slocum was startled, but covered his astonishment. The Gila Rangers all rode with him to where he had tethered his horse. He noticed how they circled him, always some-one on either side and a couple behind, as if they were herding him. But he saw a trail about where Walker had said it would be and began following it.

The moon had set by now, turning the land dark. Slo-cum occasionally dropped down to his hands and knees and studied the ground, but the trail remained distinct and fresh. This was not some wild lie Walker had told. There *was* a trail, maybe only two or three men, but a fresh trail.

Slocum stood, sniffed the night air, and motioned the others to silence. The faint burned odor of a dying camp-fire had alerted him. On foot, he and Walker advanced until they peered down into a sandy bowl near the edge of the canyon. Two dark shapes lay covered with blankets, a smoldering campfire at their feet.

"Only two?" whispered Slocum.

"They must have split up. We get these two, we can find the rest," Walker assured him. He motioned. The Gila Rangers split up and circled the camp. With a whoop and guns firing, they ran forward, frightening the two sleeping men.

Walker kicked away one man's pistol. The other came up with a knife, and immediately found himself staring down the barrels of two rifles.

"What's goin' on? You come to rob us? We ain't got nothin' worth takin', 'cept our horses. And you're not horse thieves, are you?"

"You robbed the bank over in Neutral. Where's the loot?"

"Don't know what you're talkin' about," said the man with the knife. He tossed it aside. "We rode down from the north. Been—"

"Liar!" shouted Walker, hitting the man with the barrel of his heavy pistol. The man fell across his blanket, dazed.

The other surged up, coming after Walker. Three of the Gila Rangers knocked him to the ground.

"You can't kill prominent bankers and get away with it. Where's the loot you took from the bank?"

"Listen, mister, we don't know nuthin' 'bout no bank robbery or killin'!"

"A likely story. We tracked you all the way from town."

Slocum thought that Walker had said that to weasel the truth from the men, then realized that Walker had no way of knowing for sure. Walker might have just come across the trail of two drifters. For all that, Slocum wondered how the Gila Rangers had gotten on the robbers' trail faster than he had.

"Where's the money?" Walker demanded.

"We don't know 'bout no money!" the man pleaded, frightened now that anger had run its course.

"String the mangy cayuses up. We'll give them a taste of Arizona justice!"

"Wait!" Slocum protested. "If they killed Reilly, we ought to take them back to town for a trial."

"Hell, Slocum, *you* tracked 'em too. Don't go soft now. They're guilty, and they're not talking, so what good are they?"

Walker turned. His men had nooses around the two drifters' necks and hoisted them astride their horses.

"If they buried the money, hanging them means you'll never find it," Slocum said.

"Pity, that," Walker said. "It wasn't our money to start with, but we think justice is more important."

The sharp cracks as two Gila Rangers slapped the rumps of the horses and caused them to bolt were followed fast by the sick crunching of necks breaking in the nooses. The two men kicked feebly and then died.

"This is the way we dish out justice, Slocum." Walker

turned and belligerently thrust out his chin, as if begging Slocum to contradict him.

"Arizona justice," Slocum muttered, knowing the sight of the two lynched men would stay with him for a long time. It always did when innocent men were killed.

6

"You could have at least brought back the bodies," Slocum said as he and Walker rode side by side into Neutral. He noticed how the townspeople eyed them, how he had gone from being a worthless loafer who couldn't get a job to someone to be feared. The Gila Rangers might call themselves vigilantes, but Slocum saw the truth was something more. Walker and his cronies held the town in a grip of fear.

"Why bother? We know they done it. We'll just sidle on up to the sheriff's desk and ask for the reward money, if there is any."

Slocum dismounted and followed Walker into Hardeen's office. The sheriff looked up, startled. Slocum wondered if he had not expected to see Walker—or Slocum riding with Walker.

"What can I do for you?" the sheriff asked.

"We upped and hung a pair of the varmints what robbed the bank," Walker said boldly. "Anyone put up a reward for solvin' that crime?"

"A man was killed," Slocum pointed out.

"A man?" Sheriff Hardeen sniffed. "If you want to go and call Seamus Reilly a man. A monster's more like it.

53

I'm happier getting the robbery solved, 'less you can say positively the men you hung also killed him."

"That'd solve a lot of problems, wouldn't it Sheriff?"

"You got a bug up your ass, Slocum?" The lawman glared at him.

"Now, now, settle down, you two," said Walker. "How much reward are we lookin' at, Sheriff?"

"Nothing. Nobody posted a red cent. And nobody much cared that Reilly was gunned down. If anything, they might take up a collection for the one that did it. He wasn't well liked, Slocum, if you hadn't figured that out for yourself."

"I had," Slocum admitted. "Still, he was a citizen and his killers ought to be brought to trial."

"Sounds like they got their necks stretched. That ought to be enough for any killer in these parts. Sorry, Walker, no reward, but a heartfelt 'thank you' from the people of Neutral is in order."

"No reward? Hell with it," Walker said. Slocum saw the man wasn't as put out as he might have been. If the Gila Rangers weren't being paid directly, and Walker had failed to pull in a reward, why was the man so cheerful?

Unless he and the others were sitting on a pile of gold coins and a wad of greenbacks stolen from Reilly's bank.

What Slocum couldn't figure out was Hardeen's part in the crime. Was the sheriff just a dupe, or was he getting a cut to look the other way?

"Come on over to the Dead Lizard, Slocum, and I'll buy you a drink, seeing as how you don't have any money," said Walker.

"Thanks, but I need to tend my horse. Meet you there in a while?"

"Don't reckon we'll go far, unless it's over to the Sundog Saloon." Walker strutted out, as if he owned the town. From the expression on Sheriff Hardeen's face, the banty rooster of a gunman just might. Slocum touched the brim of his floppy hat in the sheriff's direction and stepped back into the mounting heat of the day.

He led his horse to the stable, did a few chores to pay for the fodder, then went to find Grace. The Reilly house was on the side of the hill overlooking Neutral, about the biggest in town. He knocked on the whitewashed door and waited, wondering if she was inside. As he was about to give up hope of finding her at home, the door opened.

In spite of her red eyes and nose from crying, she was still about the most lovely creature Slocum had ever seen.

"John, you're back. What happened?"

He stepped in. He wanted to kiss her, but she turned from him. He knew this wasn't time for anything but a quick summary of what had gone on.

"So the Gila Rangers hanged those two men, without any evidence at all?" She dabbed at her eyes and nose with a lace handkerchief.

"I don't think they had ever been to Neutral, much less held up the bank or killed your pa," Slocum said. "Walker found a pair of scapegoats, nothing more."

"You think he's the one, don't you? Walker?"

"Yep."

Grace said nothing for long minutes. She stared out the front window, down the hill toward the slowly dying boomtown. When she spoke, it took Slocum a couple seconds to understand what she was saying.

"He's much better."

"Tolliver?"

"Yes, he can sit up and take solid food now. I have to feed him, you see, but he's tolerating it well."

"He's lucky to have you nursing him back to health," Slocum said. "When does Dr. Martin think he'll be able to ride?"

"Not for another week, perhaps two. There is danger Clay might begin bleeding inside again."

"What are you going to do, Grace? Now that your pa's dead?"

Again she seemed lost in thought. She finally smiled a little and answered. "While I can't run the bank—and who would ever deposit money in a bank run by a woman?—there is some hope. I telegraphed my Uncle Matthew, and he will arrive in a few days. It seems he was already on his way here."

"Had your pa wired him to come?"

"Uncle Matthew did not say. Perhaps it is simply my luck turning for the better."

"Does he know anything about banking?"

"Oh, yes, he and my father started several banks together out in California. If anything, Uncle Matthew is even more astute when it comes to lending money."

"It might be best to sell him your interest in the bank and go somewhere else."

"Where, John? Other than Uncle Matthew, I don't have any relatives."

That set Slocum to thinking along paths he preferred to avoid. Grace was a lovely woman, one any man would be proud to marry. But he and Grace married, living together? He felt as if a weight had settled on him, pinning him to the ground. The sunset held almost as much interest for Slocum as the sunrise. He was always willing to ride to see what lay beyond either. With a wife, he wouldn't be able to take off like that.

Still, a small ranch, maybe in Colorado, would provide everything they would need to live. He had been raised to be a farmer. Although he had never been as good as his brother Robert, he was no slouch. If there was a chance at hunting, no wife of his would ever go hungry.

But the loss of freedom . . .

"John? John! Are you all right? You seemed to just . . . go away."

"I'm fine. I wanted to be sure you were too."

"Thank you so much. Would you walk me back into town? I want to see how Clay is doing."

"All right," Slocum said, feeling a trifle guilty that he wasn't thinking of his partner too. They went down the hill to the surgery. Clay Tolliver was sleeping. Grace decided to stay, and Slocum had other plans.

He glanced into the Dead Lizard, hunting for Walker and the other Gila Rangers. The man was nowhere to be seen, but the short, well-dressed gent Slocum had come across a couple times before held up the corner of the bar. Slocum eyed him carefully, wondering what he found suspicious about him.

"Come on in, Slocum," the man called. "I'll buy you a drink."

Slocum wasn't going to refuse. He sat down at a nearby table, back to the wall, while the short man continued to prop his elbow against the bar.

"We've never been properly introduced," the man said. "Yarrow's my name." Slocum shook the hand, noticing the hard calluses. For all the fancy dress, this wasn't a soft man. Not a gambler. The calluses weren't in the right places.

"How is it you know me?" Slocum asked.

"Can't say that I do, but every time something important happens in Neutral, you are there in the middle of it. You find them killers, the ones that shot Seamus Reilly?"

"Met up with Walker and the Gila Rangers out on the trail," Slocum said carefully. "They think they found the owlhoots responsible."

"Strung 'em up, from what I hear."

"You heard right." Slocum sipped at the whiskey. He got an increasingly uneasy feeling about Yarrow. Might be Yarrow was the right height for the man who had cut down Reilly in the bank. Slocum couldn't rightly tell. He had been thinking Walker, but Yarrow was closer to the right build, even if the murderer had not worn such fancy duds.

Might be Yarrow had bank-robbing clothes, and then more elaborate ones for everyday use.

"Doesn't sound as if you think Walker got the right men."

"I'm a novice when it comes to law-enforcing. Sheriff Hardeen agreed with Walker that those were the men."

"Do tell. Then there's no reward posted for the robbers—the killers?"

"None."

Slocum wondered at Yarrow's interest. If the man was a bounty hunter, he was out of luck. Walker would have claimed any reward—and there had not been one. If Yarrow was responsible for Reilly's murder, he must think he'd gotten away scot-free, two innocent men swinging from the limb of a cottonwood out in the mountains. Somehow, Slocum did not feel that Yarrow rejoiced at outwitting the law. He couldn't figure out what Yarrow was after.

But Slocum knew deep down in his gut that it was something.

Maybe Yarrow had a gang and wanted to move in on Walker's?

"Got to mosey on," Slocum said. "Thanks for the drink."

"Any time, Slocum, any time. You just look me up."

"I'll do that, Yarrow. Count on it." With that Slocum left the Dead Lizard and stepped into the furnace-hot street. He almost turned and went back inside. The oppressive heat wore him down and made him yearn for places farther north.

Like in Colorado? Maybe with Grace?

Slocum shook himself and headed for the next saloon. The Sundog was empty, save for the barkeep sleeping on the bar. Beyond it was the Lost Dutchman Dance Hall.

The piano had been reduced to splinters and the pieces stacked in the corner. Two or three chairs were intact. The entire main room of the saloon had been the scene of a big fight recently. Or not so recently. The owner might never replace any of the broken chairs or tables—or pianos.

What caught Slocum's eye wasn't the destruction inside, but the back door closing. He hurried around the saloon in time to see Walker and one of his henchmen standing close together and talking in guarded tones. The two began speaking more heatedly until Walker angrily gestured, then shoved the other man. He crashed into a wall and started for his six-shooter.

Walker punched him hard in the belly and doubled him over. Then Walker grabbed the man by the shoulders and straightened him so he could stare straight into the taller man's face.

"You'll do as you're told," Walker said. "Nobody's cuttin' out on me, not now."

"But you said we could go when we wanted. It's gettin' too hot for me."

"It's mighty cool six feet under. Now get your ass on your saddle and ride."

Walker turned his back on his henchman and stalked off. Slocum waited to see if the man shot Walker in the back. He saw the thought go through the man's head, then vanish. Shoulders slumped, spirit broken, the man followed after his boss.

Slocum headed for the stables. He wanted to follow and find out what had riled Walker so much that he had threatened his own man. As Slocum crossed the street, he was aware of eyes watching his every move. He stopped and stared back at Yarrow. The natty man leaned against a rail, looking for all the world like a well-dressed crow on a rail fence, searching for an eye to peck out.

Slocum nodded in the man's direction, and got a similar

response. He tried not to speed up, but wasn't sure he succeeded. Appearing in a hurry while Yarrow scrutinized his every move would only bring out questions and trouble.

Slocum saddled and rode out the back of the stable, then reconsidered. With Yarrow so intent on his actions, it wouldn't do to look like he was sneaking around. Slocum turned his pony's face and rode into the middle of the main street. A smile crossed Slocum's face. Yarrow had expected him to sneak out of town, and must be watching the rear of the buildings along the main street. Putting his heels to his horse's flanks, Slocum galloped out of Neutral, then slowed a half mile outside of town.

Things got harder for Slocum now. Coming across Walker would hardly work after pointedly turning down the man's offer to join the Gila Rangers. Slocum got off the road and cut across country, keeping the dusty twin ruts that passed for a stagecoach route in sight until he spotted four other riders. He turned cautious, and was glad for it.

Riding parallel to the men on the road worked until they cut into the countryside, heading for a pile of boulders just ahead of Slocum. He reined in and waited, making sure of the riders' destination.

Dismounting, Slocum tethered his horse to a low-growing mesquite and advanced on foot.

Like a snake he slithered over the rocks, homing in on the sound of horses neighing and men swearing. Slocum checked the angle of the sun to make sure he did not accidentally silhouette himself against the sky, then settled down to wait.

Walker rode in a few minutes later, and motioned the scattered men over to a spot Slocum could not have chosen better. A full dozen men circled Walker, but it was obvious half of them were not sure of the man's leadership.

"You boys have done good," Walker said. "That makes you full members of the Gila Rangers."

"We ain't so sure this is a good move on our part," said one man who stood a full head taller than Walker. "Why do we want to risk our necks and then give you everything?"

"You know the reason, Utah," Walker said, going to the man and peering up at him. "I know things you don't. That makes it worth your while to throw in with us."

"You got a mighty big bunch. Divvying up any loot makes my share—or the shares for me and my two partners—mighty small."

"But there'll be more to divvy if you stick with me," Walker said.

"Not too convincing, no, sir," Utah said.

Slocum had seen the tall man before, up in Utah. Utah Jaeger had worked the stagecoach routes until the law came down hard on him and ran him out of the state.

"I know what'll be on each and every stage," Walker bragged. "Why waste time lifting pocket watches from peddlers when you can get greenbacks and even gold?"

"Payroll for Fort Carleton?" asked Utah.

"Might be. Takin' that would be a whale of a lot more lucrative than petty thievin' off passengers when the Butterfield don't ship anything."

"You can find this out? No fooling?"

"No fooling."

"Then I reckon me and my boys are in. Put 'er there." Utah thrust out his hand. Walker shook it hard to seal their deal, then stepped back and waved in Slocum's direction.

"Come on in!" Walker called.

Slocum froze when he heard boots scraping on the rock behind him.

7

Slocum wanted to bolt like a rabbit, but instead froze like a deer hearing an approaching hunter. He concentrated on fading into the rough stone under him, and it must have worked. Three men scrambled over the rocks not five feet from him. They never saw him.

Dropping to the ground, the trio of sentries went to Walker.

"Howdy, Boss," said the one Slocum remembered as Slim. "Fancy us comin' on you like this." The man winked broadly and laughed. Walker sneered and turned from him. Utah sucked in his breath, and then let it out slowly. He saw how close to being shot in the back he had come. Walker had had his snipers stationed in the rocks, waiting to see how the negotiations went.

"Glad to be in the Gila Rangers," Utah said.

Slocum wiped at rivers of sweat creeping down his forehead and threatening to run into his eyes. Providence had been on his side this time. He considered slipping away, but decided against it. Too many men below were looking uneasy. Antsy men tended to shoot at anything that moved.

Walker, Utah, Slim, and the rest talked for some time,

but Slocum could not hear what they said. Walker drew maps in the dirt, then quickly erased them as if he'd laid out an attack worthy of Robert E. Lee and wanted to keep troop movements secret. From the way the man pointed, segmenting the group around him, Slocum thought Walker might be plotting more than one robbery. The territory would ring like a bell in response if Walker kept up his crime wave. How long before the territorial governor took note and moved in marshals?

It might put Neutral back on the map, for a spell. When Walker either left the area or was caught and put in Yuma Penitentiary over on the Colorado River, the town would probably dry up and blow away. Such notoriety had a way of sucking up whatever life juices remained, leaving behind only a dried husk.

Slocum did not consider Neutral's demise to be much of a loss.

He wiggled a few inches back, then waited to see if anyone had noticed. The meeting below broke up. Men mounted and rode deeper into the mountains. Walker and Utah continued talking in guarded tones for another few minutes. Then Utah rode off with a few of his men trailing behind. This left Walker, Slim, and three others. Slocum kept creeping away, but froze when Walker's hand flashed for his six-shooter.

The outlaw drew, cocked, and aimed it directly between the eyes of the man he had argued with back in Neutral.

"You remember what I said about it being a mite cooler six feet under?"

"Hey, Walker, calm down," the man said, putting his hands in front of him as if to push away the Gila Rangers' leader. "You said I could ride on whenever I wanted. You convinced me that's not a smart thing to do right now, when things are startin' to move."

"You're right about that. Even *thinkin'* on it ain't so smart, and you been doin' too much thinkin'.."

Slocum flinched when Walker's gun went off. The bullet caught his henchman smack between the eyes. The man's head snapped back, and he stared upward at the cloudless blue Arizona sky for a moment. Then he slumped bonelessly.

"You want we should bury him, Boss?"

"Don't bother, Slim. I was lyin' 'bout it bein' any cooler in a grave. Where he's gone, it's a damn sight hotter 'n here!"

They laughed, got their horses, and rode away, leaving the man for the buzzards and coyotes.

Slocum saw the kind of men he was up against. It would make it easier when the time came for him to pull the trigger on them. Dusting himself off, Slocum backtracked and then circled to where he had left his horse. He made sure the Gila Rangers had not left snipers to kill him, then mounted and rode straight to Neutral.

"Come on in and have a drink, Slocum. You look mighty dusty."

Slocum dismounted in front of the Dead Lizard Dance Hall. Yarrow was being mighty friendly for no good reason. That meant he wanted something Slocum had. Since Slocum was still hunting for a pair of nickels to rub together, that meant Yarrow sought information.

Slocum wasn't inclined to share what he had learned of the Gila Rangers with anyone, especially a man with as mysterious an aspect about him as Yarrow. For all Slocum knew, Yarrow might be part of the gang assigned to ferreting out any leaks.

"Thank you kindly," Slocum said. He was willing to drink, but only to a point. He had to watch his tongue. "Think the barkeep's got any food sitting out?"

"We'll see what he can rustle up."

Slocum joined Yarrow in the cooler, dimmer bar and sat heavily. He was dog-tired from spying on Walker. His thoughts got jumbled when he tried to figure how to rob the robbers and how to keep from revealing anything important to Yarrow. The only reason he put up with the small, stylishly dressed man was the way he poured whiskey and managed to rustle up food. Without him, Slocum might have starved by now.

"You having any luck finding a job?"

"I've been in the hills, asking if any of the miners need a mucker," Slocum lied. "Backbreaking work, but I'm getting desperate."

"Most of the miners wouldn't give you room and board along with a job like that. You'd lose money."

"If I didn't starve first. I found most want me to work a week or two before they'd pay. How's a body supposed to get along until then?"

"The general store owner's not inclined to give credit." Yarrow laughed. "I know. I asked."

"What is your business in these parts, Yarrow?" Slocum decided it was time to turn the tables and see how well Yarrow danced around answering.

"You might say I am an adjustor."

"What's that?"

"I take a look at what's wrong and make it right. The deeds for the land around Neutral, for instance, are a real mess. Might take a good lawyer months to be sure everyone's title is properly recorded and legally registered."

"You a lawyer?"

Yarrow took a drink. His eyes danced. "I work for a lawyer. You ever do that?"

"Once," Slocum said. "I got over it."

Yarrow laughed and slapped his thigh. "I do like you, Slocum. You got a sense of humor that appeals to me."

"You gonna be in Neutral very long?" Slocum asked. Seeing the lie forming in Yarrow's eyes, Slocum went on. "I'd hate to see my obliging river of whiskey dry up."

"Yes, indeed, I do like your sense of humor."

For a spell Slocum ate the roast beef sandwich laced with horseradish furnished by the barkeep and drank the whiskey. Yarrow had lapsed into deep thought, as if considering what to do with Slocum. His musings were interrupted when Sheriff Hardeen came into the saloon.

Hardeen saw Slocum and almost backed out. But he seemed to brace up and get some spine, then came on in and bellied up to the bar.

"Whiskey," the sheriff ordered. Slocum saw the barkeep gave the lawman some of the bar stock, nothing but trade whiskey made with gunpowder, nitric acid, and fermented fruit. The bottle Yarrow had gotten from the bartender was real whiskey, if not *good* real whiskey.

"You know the sheriff?" asked Yarrow.

Slocum shook his head. "Don't make it a habit getting to know the local law." The way Yarrow laughed at this turned Slocum even more wary since he could not figure out what the man was driving at.

Hardeen waved to someone out in the street, then went back to nursing his trade whiskey. Slocum tried to see who had drawn the sheriff's attention, but couldn't. He pushed back from the table and stood.

"Much obliged again, Yarrow. One of these days I'll return the favor."

"I'm sure you will, Slocum, I'm sure you will." Yarrow raised his glass in a mocking toast, then downed the whiskey in a gulp. Slocum left, wondering what he had gotten himself mixed up in. Yarrow didn't fit. Hardeen didn't either.

Slocum thought about going to the doctor's office and seeing how Tolliver was getting along. It had been a spell since he had checked on his partner, but now Slocum saw who had waved to the sheriff. Walker and three of the Gila Rangers rode fast out of town, going west. Slocum moseyed over to the Butterfield office and poked his head inside. The station agent had propped himself in the chair, feet on his dusty desk, head tipped to one side as he snored.

Rather than wake him, Slocum went to the man's desk and rummaged through the papers until he found the daily stagecoach schedule. He sucked in his breath when he saw a stage was due in at sundown.

Remembering what Walker had said to Utah galvanized Slocum into action. Whatever Walker's source of information, this was one of the stages the Gila Rangers were going to rob. Slocum felt it in his bones. He hurried to the stable and saddled his tired horse. He only took enough time to be certain the horse had drunk its fill. The Arizona desert was mighty dry and mighty deadly without enough water.

As he rode from town, Slocum saw Yarrow perched on a rail, again watching everything that went on in town. Slocum waved, but Yarrow was intent on something else and did not respond. That was just as well. Whatever the man really did, it went far beyond land deeds and working for a lawyer.

The ride to the west along the Gila Road proved strenuous, and Slocum's horse began to flag almost immediately. Slocum slowed to a walk, changed gait several times, dismounted and walked a half mile, then repeated so the horse had a chance to rest. Somehow, Slocum knew he would miss something important if he permitted the horse simply to cool off in the dubious shade of a mesquite or the tall cut bank of an arroyo.

All the places along the road he and Tolliver had identified as likely places for a holdup came to him. Picturing the land in his mind's eye, Slocum cut across the desert, wending in and out of the curious candelabralike saguaros, and finally came to a rise overlooking the main Gila Road.

He was in time to see four armed, masked men holding up the stagecoach. They had pushed a few large rocks into the road to stop the stage, then jumped out with leveled six-shooters when the shotgun messenger jumped down to do something about the blocked road.

Slocum shook his head in dismay. The road agents cut down the guard without giving him a chance to surrender. They were cold-blooded killers out in the burning-hot desert. This tempered his resolve to take whatever they stole from the stagecoach and keep it for himself.

He would be careful spreading the money around. Paying off Dr. Martin was at the top of the list, but he doubted the rummy of a doctor would boast much about the source of his newfound wealth. A few more dollars could be spent judiciously for supplies. Then he and Tolliver could hightail it from Neutral.

Even as that thought went through his head, he knew he had to consider Grace Reilly. She was something special to him, but what woman deserved being on the run with two broken-down cowboys chased at every turn by the law?

"Git on along, you hear?" shouted the road agent's leader. Slocum recognized Walker's voice immediately. The stagecoach lumbered along, picked up speed, and was soon around a bend in the road, making good time for Neutral to report the crime.

Slocum wondered which direction Walker would head. If the man had any sense, he would go straight south to lose himself in Mexico amid the bottles of tequila and pretty *señoritas*. Somehow, it didn't come as much of a surprise when Walker and his men rode north into the foothills. They had a camp up there, Slocum knew.

He had almost caught them there the other night, when he had inadvertently been responsible for the deaths of the two drifters. Slocum had to believe Walker would never have strung the two up if he himself had not been there to witness how eager for Arizona justice Walker and the Gila Rangers were.

Out in the desert, tracking them was more difficult because he did not want to be spotted, but the Gila Rangers quickly found a trail winding up into the mountains that took them out of direct observation of their backtrail. Slocum rode along, wary of any outlaw posted as a guard. Mile after mile he rode without seeing any hint that Walker had posted sentries along his trail.

That meant either that Walker was arrogant *and* stupid, or that no one bothered the Gila Rangers. The former might be right, but Slocum figured the latter was definitely so. He had yet to understand Sheriff Hardeen's role in the robberies, if there was one. The man might be slow-witted and not see his personal vigilante army was carrying out the robberies, or he might be scared out of his wits by them.

Or he might give Walker the protection afforded by a sheriff. Hardeen might get a cut of everything the Gila Rangers stole in return for protection.

It hardly mattered since Slocum intended to steal from all the thieves, no matter who they were. If he picked Hardeen's pocket along with Walker's, how much worse could that be?

The sun dipped quickly behind the mountains, resulting in another breathtaking Arizona sunset Slocum was in no mood to appreciate. His horse stumbled and wobbled under him, but he kept the beast moving until darkness fell. Slocum was worried that the horse might step in a hole and break a leg in the dark. He dismounted and walked the horse up the steep slope until he came to a small, grassy meadow that promised water.

The horse balked and refused to go farther. Slocum let the horse graze while he scouted the area. This was the sort of place he would usually pitch camp. Unless Walker had somewhere higher up that gave a better view of the trail, he probably camped here too.

The sound of splashing water amid the trees followed

by bawdy laughter told Slocum he had found the Gila
Rangers. Scrub oak and some pinyon grew tall enough to
hide his advance. Each footstep was done with great care
to keep from breaking a twig and betraying himself. The
Gila Rangers were relaxing, but that didn't mean they had
gone deaf—or were less suspicious than before. He
reached the edge of the clearing and peered out.

Again he was astounded at Walker's confidence. The
leader of the Gila Rangers had not posted any guards here
either.

The small, deep pool of clear water fed by mountain
runoff was filled with men bathing, splashing one another
and making vulgar jokes. Slocum ignored what they did,
and hunted for where they had stashed their six-shooters.
Some kept them by the edge of the pool. Others had left
their weapons in camp. There were still too many for Slocum to take on, not that he wanted to.

Moving like a shadow within a shadow, Slocum came
to a clearing where three campfires burned low and
banked. At one sat Walker and Utah, the loot from the
stagecoach robbery in piles on the ground in front of
them.

How Slocum was going to rob them when they were
divvying it up was a problem he had to solve and fast.

8

"You think the split's fair?" asked Walker.

"Not as much as I'd've got on my own." Utah Jaeger spat into the fire, which sizzled and popped. A thin spiral of steam rose, to be carried away into the night air. Utah wiped his mouth and looked sidewise at Walker. "Me and my men will take our cut and move on, Walker. Can't see how throwin' in with you helps us one little bit."

"Sorry to hear you say that, Utah."

Slocum saw the way Walker gathered the piles of loot and shoved them off to one side, as if he didn't want to divvy it up any more. Utah shifted his weight slightly, his hand going to his six-shooter when he saw how Walker responded to his ultimatum. He never had a chance to back up his intention to move on—with his share of the booty. Both his partners had their hoglegs out and blasted him in the back before he could clear leather.

Even after Utah fell facedown in the dirt, his two former partners kept firing. A smirk on Walker's face told Slocum how much the outlaw enjoyed this double-dealing. Having a man's own partners turn on him was just the thing to make Walker happy, that and taking the cut of the loot that ought to have gone to Utah Jaeger.

"You gents finished?" Walker asked when both men's hammers fell on emptied chambers.

"Reckon so, Mr. Walker. You can go on and split Utah's share 'tween us. We done what you asked." One came up and kicked his dead partner in the ribs, to make sure there wasn't any life left in his bullet-riddled body. The other watched in silence, letting his friend do the talking. "First time I ever double-crossed a partner, 'specially one as good as Utah."

"You won't be doin' that again any time soon," Walker said.

"Nope. This was a one-time occurrence. We can assure you of that, Mr. Walker."

As the two men reloaded their pistols, Slocum saw why they wouldn't be crossing Walker the way they had their former partner. From behind them rose rifle barrels. The sharp reports and the men's sharp gasps of pain and surprise as they died insured they had done their last crooked deed.

"Get 'em outta camp 'fore they start to smell worse 'n they do now," Walker said. Slim and another of the Gila Rangers came into the campfire light, laid down their rifles, and then grunted as they dragged the three bodies out of sight in the woods.

Slocum went cold inside watching such murder. Walker had played with Utah like a cat with a mouse. Then he had convinced the man's two partners to turn on him, before having them cut down from ambush. Walker was one dangerous owlhoot.

Chuckling as he worked, Walker counted the greenbacks that had been split into separate piles. Now they were all in front of him where he could scoop them into one large stack. He finished a second count, then stuffed the bills into a canvas bag and looked around. Slocum froze, not moving a muscle. Walker took the bag into the darkness just beyond the circle of light where Slocum could see, then returned a few minutes later without the bag.

He had hidden it somewhere in the wooded area, and Walker wasn't going to cut his fellow Gila Rangers in on the loot. Slocum backed away, then hurried off, knowing he could never find the bag of greenbacks from the stagecoach robbery without alerting Walker or his men. He memorized the terrain as he went, intending to come back later and search for the money.

Who knows? He might find more than that one bag of loot. Walker didn't seem the type to cut his men in on much from any robbery. He doled out enough to keep them happy, keeping the biggest portion for himself. It was up to Slocum to find the money and relieve Walker of the burden of figuring out how to spend it all.

Slocum walked his horse a couple miles, then rode very slowly, letting the horse pick its way down the steep mountain trail. Now and then Slocum dismounted, rested his horse, and waited to see if any of the Gila Rangers followed. None did. He was back in Neutral by sunrise, tired and making plans for how he would spend all the money he was going to steal from Walker.

"Sleepyhead," said the soft, musical voice. Slocum came awake, hand on his Colt Navy, then relaxed when he saw Grace standing in the stall where he had slept.

"What time is it?"

"Past noon. You'll never make any money sleeping away the day. I'm surprised Mr. Summers didn't wake you."

The livery owner had done his work and then left before Slocum had come back. The empty stalls told more about the condition of Neutral than anything else. Other than Slocum's and Tolliver's, Leon Summers had only one horse boarded in the stable.

"Got in late," Slocum said. "Or real early, depending on how you look at it."

"I've missed you," she said, dropping into the straw beside him. Grace lay back, hands under her head and staring straight up. Sunlight poured through the cracks in the wall and, filtered by dust, turned her into some gauzy, angelic figure. Slocum saw the way her breasts rose and fell gently, and began arguing with himself about what to tell her of his scheme to rob the robbers.

He decided to tell Grace what he intended, how he had found Walker's stash and everything about the Gila Rangers, but she never gave him a chance.

"He's so much better, John. He's recovering nicely."

"Tolliver?"

"Yes, silly. Who else?" asked Grace. She smiled and sat up. "Let's go see him. You'll be surprised at how well he is doing. Dr. Martin did a fine job patching him up."

"Tolliver's a tough old bastard," Slocum said. "It's hard to keep him down."

"Not so old," Grace said. "And he is certainly *not* a bastard."

Slocum wondered at her piqued retort. She could be so prim at times, so wanton at others. Figuring her out was more than Slocum could do with lack of sleep and an even greater lack of food.

They went into Dr. Martin's surgery to find Clay Tolliver propped up in bed. He had been expertly bandaged around the chest and some color had returned to his face.

"My favorite nurse!" he called, reaching out to Grace. He peered past her to Slocum as she gave him a gentle hug. "Don't know what I'd've done without this little lady. She keeps changin' my wrappin's when that old dog of a doctor is so drunk he don't know what he's doin'."

"She's a good nurse," Slocum said, wanting to talk to Tolliver alone about other things. He had to let him know about the scheme to rob the robbers.

"I'll be up and ridin' in another week, John. We got places to go and things to do then?"

"Maybe before. You remember the little deal we talked about on the way into town?"

"I certainly do."

"I found the mother lode and need to do some quick mining on it before it vanishes. The location's changed a mite, but it's all the richer for the new vein."

"Whatever are you two talking about?" asked Grace.

"Nothing to worry your pretty little head over," Tolliver said. "What I need to know is how long my shift will be at the bank."

"What are you talking about?" demanded Slocum.

"She didn't tell you? See how it is with her? Slocum, I have a job at the bank as a guard. Grace'll fix me up with a chair in one corner. I can sit there with a scattergun 'cross my knees and guard the bank. There's no reason it ought to be robbed like it was before."

"The other guards couldn't stop the robbers," Slocum said, shying away from actually naming Walker and the rest of the Gila Rangers as the thieves. "Truth to tell, I'm not sure what happened to them once the shooting started."

"I know what happened," Grace said in disgust. "Clay will not abandon the bank or its customers like that. This gives him the chance to earn some money *and* recuperate."

Slocum wasn't sure what he thought of this. Grace could have offered *him* the job, but he had never come out and asked. He had been too busy following Walker's trail and finding out who the real crooks were in this county.

"Might even get Sheriff Hardeen to deputize me," Tolliver said. "Wouldn't that be a delight? Folks back home'd never believe ole Clay Tolliver ended up a deputy sheriff out in Arizona Territory."

Tolliver swung his legs over the edge of the bed. Slocum waited for him to fall flat on his face, but to his surprise Tolliver had recuperated enough to take a few halting steps. Grace hurried to his side to help him walk, but he pushed her away.

"Need to practice doin' what any year-old child can do. Still weak, but gettin' better by the day."

"Standing guard isn't a good idea," Slocum said.

"Nonsense, just the thing the doctor ordered. If ole Doc Martin was ever sober enough to order it, that is." Tolliver laughed as he strapped on his six-gun. "Let's get over to the bank. Time's a'wastin', and we don't want the crooks to try again. Not now."

"What do you mean?" Slocum turned suspicious.

"Oh, nothing, John, not really," Grace said. "Don't be so distrustful. The bank's had a bit of luck since the robbery. Two mines have struck new veins of gold, and we have the nuggets and gold dust in the vault now."

"You know the combination? I thought only your pa could open the safe."

"I had it reset. *I* know it, and when my Uncle Matthew gets here, I'll let him know it too."

"Her uncle's due any time now," Tolliver said, pulling on his boots. When he stood he wobbled a mite. Otherwise, Slocum would never have known the man had been injured. Tolliver put on a new white shirt that hid the bandages around his chest, and his pants were cleaner than Slocum ever remembered seeing them.

"I washed them for him. It was the least I could do," Grace said when she saw Slocum staring in wonder at his partner.

Slocum shrugged it off. It was nothing he had not expected. Grace needed a bird with a broken wing to nurture after her pa was gunned down, and Clay Tolliver filled the bill perfectly. He ate up her attention, once he regained consciousness, and lavished obvious compliments on her to keep her happy.

Slocum knew Tolliver would be even happier when he stole the Gila Rangers' loot.

The three made their way slowly from Dr. Martin's office to the bank. Slocum saw Yarrow watching from the boardwalk in front of the Dead Lizard Dance Hall. Farther down the street, at the Rusty Bucket Saloon, Sheriff Hardeen and one of the Gila Rangers also watched the slow walk to the bank.

"Tuckered me out more 'n I thought," Tolliver admitted as they made it into the cool lobby of the adobe bank. He sank into the chair, which was already in one corner of the lobby. Two tellers looked at him skeptically. The mistrust was replaced by outright animosity when Grace handed Tolliver a shotgun.

She addressed the tellers. "Mr. Tolliver will stand guard for us. He is quite expert with this weapon and will forestall any new robbery attempt." She clapped her hands to show her approval of this capital notion. The tellers were slower to join in. Slocum only watched and shook his head. Tolliver was as weak as a kitten. He might pull the triggers on the double-barreled shotgun, but in a real fight he'd be worthless.

"You might think on getting someone else in here to help him out," Slocum said quietly to Grace. She looked up at him.

"You mean you aren't going to stay too? Why, John, I thought this was a perfect opportunity to hire both of you."

Slocum pushed aside the confusion boiling inside. He needed a job, and Grace was willing to give it to him. The very job he had considered when he rode into town, in fact. But how could he stand duty with Tolliver while the bank was open and still have a chance of finding and taking the Gila Rangers' stolen loot? One or the other was possible, but he could not do both.

If he didn't drop from exhaustion trying to reach the road agents' camp, his horse would.

"I don't need him wet-nursin' me," Tolliver protested, seeing what Slocum's dilemma actually was. "Let me get some confidence back, will you, Grace?"

"But, Clay, you—"

The front door of the bank slammed open. For a moment, Slocum thought a gust of wind had done the trick. Then he saw a bulky man step forward. His shoulders brushed the doorjambs on either side and he had to duck when he entered the bank. A giant of a man, going bald but with a shock of carrot-red hair still on top, he looked around and then bellowed, "Where's my niece? Where's Grace Reilly?"

"Uncle Matthew!" Grace rushed to him and threw her arms around his neck. He picked her up and whirled her around like a little girl.

"You haven't grown a bit since I saw you last year, my sweet colleen, except possibly you've grown lovelier. You are about the prettiest thing this side of the Mississippi."

"Only on *this* side, Uncle Matthew?" she teased.

"You're the prettiest girl from here all the way back to Ireland!" he declared.

"Reckon I still have a job?" asked Tolliver, indicating the bull of a man.

"You won't if you have to fight him for it," Slocum said dryly.

"Uncle Matthew, I want you to meet the two men who stopped one robbery, the one before Papa was . . ."

"Before them owlhoots murdered him," Matthew Reilly finished harshly for his niece. "No need to mince words, girl. Tell it like it is. Toughens the spirit for the hard work ahead."

"Yes, Uncle," she said. Tears welled in her eyes, but she tried to hide them.

"No need to be so harsh with her," Slocum said. "She's had a loss. She was here when her pa was shot down."

"Seamus was a fool. Always had been. I told him he would come to no good. Well, things are going to change around here. We will run this bank as it ought to be run, not as some charitable venture doling out money left and right."

"Are we talking about the same Seamus Reilly?" asked Tolliver. "The one I heard of would use his walking stick to beat away a beggar going for a coin dropped in the street."

"He was soft and he allowed others to be also," Matthew Reilly said. "Take them, for example." He pointed to the two tellers in their boxes. "Why do we need *two* tellers?"

"In case there is enough business," Grace began. She fell silent when his fiery gaze fixed on her.

"Wrong. There were two because Seamus was too kind-hearted to fire one. *That* one." Reilly pointed to the older of the tellers. "You're fired. Clear out of here. Now!"

"Why him?" asked Grace.

"He is older and is probably paid more as a result. Wages, my girl. Never pay your employees too well. They will come to despise you for such charity."

"Seems to me," drawled Clay Tolliver, "your employees can come to hate you for other reasons even easier."

"Who might you be again?"

"Guard," Tolliver said.

"We do not require your services any longer," Reilly said haughtily. He hooked his thumbs in the arm holes of his vest and looked down the length of his bulbous nose at Tolliver. "From your puny condition, I am not sure anyone ever needed them."

Before Tolliver could protest, Slocum took him by the arm and steered him from the bank.

"Let the dust settle a spell," Slocum advised. "We can worry about getting you back in as guard later."

"But Grace! What about her? He is walking all over her. She owns the bank!"

"No miner this side of the San Carlos River would put a plugged nickel in a bank run by a woman," Slocum said. "She can collect the profits, but her uncle has to run the bank."

"Run it? Run it into the ground, you mean! He's even worse than her father!"

Slocum wasn't up to arguing with his partner over what looked to be the truth.

9

"Son of a bitch," grumbled Clay Tolliver. He propped himself against the eastern wall outside Dr. Martin's office, in the afternoon shade and fanned himself with a week-old, yellowed front page from the *El Paso Times*.

Slocum looked at his partner and wondered what he was talking about. He held his tongue and waited. Tolliver was not the kind of man to keep to himself very long.

"That Matthew Reilly really gets my goat. Imagine firin' me, and I hadn't even been on the job ten minutes."

"That's all that's eating at you?" Slocum shook his head. The man had been close to death. If Slocum had been in Tolliver's boots, he would have been champing at the bit to get even with the robbers who'd done the shooting—with Walker and the Gila Rangers. From all appearances, something other than revenge took up space in Tolliver's head and occupied his thoughts.

From all Slocum could tell, Tolliver's memory was vague on what had happened in the bank when he was gunned down. And it got even vaguer about what had happened afterward, during his recuperation. Tolliver always brightened when Grace came by, but he never discussed the woman's visits, or even seemed to know she had made any call on him other than noting how she had bandaged him now and then.

"How strong are you?" Slocum asked. "You think you can ride?" He didn't want to push Tolliver until he was ready for the rigors of the Arizona desert in midsummer. At the best of times, it took a toll on any man.

"With the best of 'em," Tolliver boasted. "I'm getting antsy sittin' and watchin' people come and go." He spat. "Mostly goin', from the look of Neutral."

Slocum saw one permanent feature that he was almost getting used to. The dapper Yarrow watched them, as if he were a cat and they were birds waiting to be his dinner. Yarrow never ran and hid like Sheriff Hardeen when Slocum approached him, and he always offered a drink and even food. For that Slocum could not fault the man. But why was he in Neutral? Asking around had quickly confirmed what Slocum had suspected about Yarrow.

Yarrow had said he worked for a lawyer going over land deeds, but the man had not spent much time in the records office. He and his two sidekicks rode out of town fairly often, only to return in a few hours. They never strayed, and they hardly stayed. Slocum couldn't make heads or tails of it.

"Where are his partners right now?" Slocum wondered aloud. He had not seen them since they'd returned to Neutral sometime after dawn.

"Who's that?"

"Name's Yarrow. He doesn't do much but sit and watch."

"Just like me, eh?" Tolliver laughed. "Well, I'm sick and tired of bein' sick and tired. What were you anglin' to say, Slocum?"

Slocum pushed aside the question about what Yarrow's partners did while the man spied on everyone else in Neutral. They seemed to vanish until he summoned them to go riding out on some mysterious mission.

"You know we talked about robbing the stagecoach?"

"And the bank. That looks better to me all the time, just to get back at Reilly!"

"I have a better idea. How about robbing the robbers?"

"Sounds like a decent notion, Slocum. You always were a thinker. You sayin' we go out and find them?"

"The Gila Rangers are a vigilante group. Can't tell if the sheriff works for them, with them, or is just too dumb to know they're behind all the robberies."

"Heard Grace say something about the Gila Rangers. Don't remember what it was. Not exactly."

"We don't have to find their camp. Already did that." Slocum looked hard at Tolliver, judging his partner's strength and resolve. Tolliver was a good man, but the bullet wound had done things to him, changing him in ways Slocum couldn't figure. He had seen men injured as badly as Tolliver turn cautious and even fearful.

"And?" coaxed Tolliver. "You know where they hide their booty?"

"I know where Walker hid some of it. The man isn't likely to squirrel away his cut in a dozen places, so if we find where he put the loot from the stagecoach robbery, we'll probably get more than we can imagine."

"Sounds good to me. Let's go!" Tolliver used the wall to stand before he took a shaky step or two. Then he strengthened and headed for the livery.

Slocum had been taking care of Tolliver's horse, but the temptation had been great to sell it for the few miserable dollars it would bring. Now he was glad he had fed and watered the animal. As they walked, Tolliver checked his six-gun. He glanced at Slocum and shot him a feral grin.

This was more like the partner Slocum knew, and it made him feel easier. The ride would take a lot of starch out of Tolliver, but the hunt for the hidden loot ought to go fast. If the Gila Rangers were out of camp.

"There," Slocum said, lifting his chin Navajo-style to indicate Walker and two others at the Sundog Saloon. "Those gents are part of the vigilantes."

"They're in town, we're in their camp. I like it, John, I truly do," said Tolliver. The man saddled his horse and climbed up. Slocum saw a shadow of pain flash across Tolliver's face, but it faded and was replaced by his infectious grin. Slocum had missed Tolliver's good humor. He took things too seriously, and needed the bright-spirited Tolliver to keep him from getting too melancholy.

"Lead on, lead us to fame and fortune!" declared Tolliver.

"Forget the fame," said Slocum. "I'll settle for the fortune."

It was close to midnight when he and Tolliver dismounted and made their way through the wooded area outside the Gila Rangers' camp. Slocum listened hard for any sound of horses, of laughter, any scent of cooking or smoldering campfires. For a few minutes, Slocum was worried that he had come to the wrong spot. Then he stepped lightly over a huge glob of fresh horse dung, scaring away flies. All around were other indications that the Gila Rangers had corralled their horses here.

"Where do you reckon they are?" asked Tolliver. He rested his hand on his six-shooter, ready to draw and fire. Slocum had never seen him quite this jumpy before. But then he was in the camp of the men who had gunned him down. "All I saw in Neutral were Walker and two of his cronies. From what you said, there must be a dozen more of the bastards."

"Out robbing other innocent folks," Slocum said. He could not care less where the vigilantes were, as long as they were somewhere else, giving him a free hand to hunt for Walker's treasure trove.

Tolliver laughed at this, but there was no humor in it.

They parted and advanced on the camp a half-dozen paces apart. Working as a team, they swept through the abandoned camp, making certain they were alone.

"Figure they'll come back any time soon? How long do you think we got, Slocum?"

"No idea. Let's make it quick." He stood in the center of the empty encampment and slowly turned in a full circle to get his bearings. He located the stand of scrub oak where he had spied on Walker when the man had had Utah and his two partners murdered. He knelt and found dark patches in the soil where blood had been spilled.

"What'd you find?"

"Just reconstructing what I saw," Slocum said. He put himself in Walker's position, then stood and strode toward a dark growth of close-spaced ponderosas and aspen. At the edge of the copse he checked the ground again for spoor.

"In here?" Tolliver eagerly crowded Slocum. "You want me to start diggin' somewhere?"

"Soon," Slocum said, irritated at Tolliver's puppy-dog eagerness. Slocum went to his hands and knees, searching the mat of fallen pine needles and leaves for a clue where Walker had gone. Small twigs had been broken. Slocum edged in that direction. Then he looked up at a tall pine and knew he had found the vigilante leader's hiding place.

"This it?" asked Tolliver.

"Must be. See the V mark carved on the tree? It's the kind of thing Walker would do to find his loot fast. Never thought he was too bright, but he is smart enough to know his limitations."

Slocum circled the tree and found freshly turned dirt amid the roots. He pointed, and Tolliver started digging like a dog after a rabbit in its burrow. Dirt flew in all directions until Slocum began to worry that Walker had outfoxed them.

Then Tolliver let out a cry of victory.

"Lookee here, John. Ain't this 'bout the purtiest sight you ever set your eyes on?" He held up a canvas bag like those used by the Butterfield Stagecoach Company to transport mail. Tolliver brushed off dirt and revealed "U.S. Mail" on the battered leather strip at the top.

"Hope it's more than business letters," Slocum said, but his heart beat a little faster too. Walker would use mail to start a fire. He would never hide it like this. When Tolliver spilled the contents onto the ground, Slocum knew they had indeed found the mother lode.

"Christ Almighty, John, there must be a thousand dollars here. It's all in greenbacks, but I don't hold that against Walker none." Tolliver ran his fingers through the scrip, picking it up and letting it flutter to the ground. Then he scooped it up and crammed it back into the stolen mail sack.

"Let me have a few dollars," Slocum said. "I'm tired of not having enough to even buy a beer."

"Here, take it, take all this!" Tolliver shoved a wad of bills at Slocum. "You think there's more around? Walker might have hidden more under some other tree. Let's give it a look and—"

"Don't get greedy," Slocum said. "This is a powerful lot of money—and it's all stolen. We can't go spending it around town without raising suspicions."

"Of the sheriff?" scoffed Tolliver. "You said he was dumber than dirt."

"Hardeen might be in Walker's hip pocket. If so, the sheriff sees us with money and tells Walker. What happens when Walker finds his personal hoard gone?"

"Maybe we ought to ride on," Tolliver said slowly, as if testing out a theory he didn't much cotton to. "No," he answered, not waiting for Slocum. "If we did that, Walker would know who stole his money and would come after us. We stay around Neutral for a while, *then* leave. Let him suspect us all he wants."

"If we don't go buying drinks for everyone in town, Walker won't know for certain." Slocum did not point out that men like Walker usually acted on suspicion rather than logic. With a dozen or more men in the Gila Rangers, he had a small army to do his bidding. What was another death or two for a man like that?

Slocum remembered vividly how Walker had gotten Utah Jaeger's friends to murder him, then had them gunned down without so much as a fare-thee-well. The man had a streak of cruelty a mile wide.

"We stick around Neutral for a while longer," Tolliver said, sounding satisfied with this. He hefted the sack and threw it over his shoulder. He staggered a little, then smiled and explained, "Dizzy with the prospect of so much money."

"Don't let it all go to your head," Slocum said. "Half is mine."

"Thanks, partner," Tolliver said, thrusting out his dirty hand. Slocum shook on it, then motioned for them to get back to where they had staked their horses. He wanted to put as much distance between here and himself as he could before Walker returned.

They cut across the edge of the Gila Rangers' camp, and had almost started into the woods, where they had left their horses, when Slocum heard the telltale sounds of iron sliding across leather.

"Down!" he cried, shoving Tolliver forward. The man stumbled and fell as hot lead ripped through the air where his head had been an instant before. Slocum scrambled for cover behind a rotting log. It wasn't much, but it was better than nothing in the darkness.

"Where're they?"

"Don't know. Across the clearing?" Slocum slid his Colt Navy from its holster and waited. When a foot-long tongue of orange flame leaped out from a spot twenty yards away, Slocum aimed and fired fast three times, saving the other three rounds for a better shot.

"You got him, Slocum. I heard him groan," crowed Tolliver.

"Winged him, didn't kill him," Slocum said, regretting the poorly aimed shots. He had given his position away for no good reason. How many Gila Rangers did he face? He had no idea, and that might be his undoing.

"You see any of them? Really *see* them?" Slocum asked.

"Movement in shadows. Wish the moon would get up and give us some light."

Slocum glanced at the sky. Clouds moved in. Even if the almost full moon gave him some light to shoot by, it did the same for the vigilantes. He was certain he and Tolliver were outnumbered. Whatever they did to get away, they had to do it fast before the Gila Rangers organized and attacked.

"Let me have your six-shooter," Slocum said.

"What? I'm not going to—"

"Give it to me. Then you take the money and hightail it. You're not up to fighting them. I am. You get to your horse and ride like hell back to town and hide the money."

"What about you? I can't leave you!"

"Do it, Tolliver. I can distract them until you're safely away. There won't be much trouble getting out of here, if I can keep them stirred up."

"That's a mighty big risk."

"We don't have time to discuss the matter," Slocum said. "Give me your six-shooter and then get the hell out of here!"

"Well, all right, but I don't like this none."

"See you back in Neutral," Slocum said, hefting Tolliver's six-gun in his left hand. It wasn't balanced properly, but it held six more rounds, shots he needed. He nodded to Tolliver, then poked his head up and fired three more times, using his partner's pistol.

Tolliver scuttled off like a crab, then used the trees for cover and ran into the thicket. Slocum counted to five, decided Tolliver would be mounting his horse about now, then got his feet under him and sprinted for a spot back toward the woods where they had pilfered Walker's cache of greenbacks.

He drew fire immediately, and some of it came from rifles. The deeper sound and the throatier whistle of the slugs ripping through the air all around lent speed to his dash. Slocum tripped and fell, got back to his feet, and used this as a chance to double back. He momentarily confused his attackers.

Seeing a shape in front of him forced Slocum to use two more rounds. The vigilante cried out and threw up his hands. A rifle dropped to the ground. Slocum used Tolliver's last round to finish off the man, then scooped up the fallen rifle.

He heard the Gila Rangers closing in from all sides.

He crouched, wondering what to do now.

10

Slocum felt like a trapped rat. He could hardly see the Gila Rangers around him, but he heard them charging like runaway freight trains. For once, he was glad he worked in darkness, though the clouds were beginning to break up and a hint of bright silver moon poked through. If it came out fully, he was a goner. They would never let him get away.

Slocum turned to his left and fired until his Colt Navy came up empty. Then he fired the last round from Tolliver's gun. Behind that single round he threw the six-shooter, clipping one outlaw on the side of the head with it.

"The varmint's not got no gun," the man cried in triumph. Slocum homed in on the voice and showed him how wrong he was. The rifle barked once, ending the man's life.

Then Slocum got an idea. He turned and fired to his left, swung and fired right. Diving for the ground, he wiggled along like a snake, hunting for any shelter he could find in the leaden firestorm over his head. The outlaws had made the mistake of coming at him from all sides. He had decoyed the ones on the right to fire on those after him on the left. When both flanks started firing, he was well under their deadly aim as they cut down one another.

This still presented him with a big problem. The men in front were alerted by all the firing. Slocum took careful aim and potted one half-exposed outlaw behind a tree trunk. The man slumped soundlessly, giving Slocum the break he needed. He wiggled and squirmed and got to the man's post. He quickly stood and waved.

"He didn't come this way!" Slocum called. "Is he coming your way?" He didn't care who believed him or who didn't. He wanted to sow discord in the Gila Rangers' rank. And he did.

It might have been a mountain thunderstorm that cut loose on that grassy meadow, but it wasn't. The outlaws fired at anything that moved. Slocum made sure he was standing stock-still and not attracting attention. Then someone he didn't recognize tried to get some order in the Gila Rangers' rank.

"Stop, stop firing, dang nab it!"

"That you, Enoch?"

"Of course it is, you mule-eared cayuse! He's got us shootin' one another. Where'd he get off to?"

"Not this way!" called Slocum, again diverting attention. He doubted he could do that much longer. The dead man at his feet had friends in this vigilante band. Someone would notice the change in voice, the way he spoke, something that would give him away.

"There!" Slocum shouted. "I see him!" He fired through the meadow, past the one who was trying to assume leadership. The man—Enoch?—screeched in anger when Slocum's slug missed him by inches. But the diversion was enough to send the vigilantes thundering off after the mythical fleeing victim.

Slocum went the other way, found his horse, and mounted. He wondered if Tolliver was already on the trail back to Neutral. If so, Slocum ought to go another way.

It would not be too long before Enoch figured out the trick and had his men on the trail. They might not know he and Tolliver had robbed Walker of his loot, but they knew something was wrong in the camp.

If they thought a lawman had found the camp, it would be like stirring up a beehive. The response would be immediate, and it would be mighty painful to anyone getting in the way of the swarm.

Slocum found the trail leading downhill, toward the Gila Road and Neutral. He cut across it, and kept moving through thicket and undergrowth until he came to a fairly open forest of pines and spruce. He rode with the downhill slope on his right, waiting for the proper time to turn uphill and then cross the mountain. If he got to the other side, he stood a chance of getting back to the Gila Road a dozen miles outside the Butterfield way station. He could get some food, buy more ammo with the money riding high in his shirt pocket, and even see that his horse was tended before heading to Neutral.

He rode through the dark forest, listening hard for sounds of pursuit. When they didn't come, Slocum got even edgier. Enoch wasn't going to let anyone escape without finding out what they were doing poking around the Gila Rangers' camp. Walker would have his ears for trophies if he didn't bring back at least one dead body.

Slocum reined back and listened even harder. All he could hear was the sound of his own heart thumping. He sniffed the air. Lathered horse, his own sweat, the deep fragrance of pines, nothing more. A new sound came. A coyote in the distance howling for his canyons-distant canine lover.

But otherwise even the wind had gone silent, and this worried Slocum.

The utter stillness felt like the calm before a major battle. He had experienced this more than once during the war, and it always meant bloodshed—and lots of it. The very world seemed frightened and hiding, unsure of itself. Slocum knew what had to be done. He put his heels into his reluctant horse's flanks and got moving, ducking now and then under low-hanging branches.

When he came out in a meadow he had a gut-sinking feeling he had somehow circled and come back to the spot where the Gila Rangers camped. Then he saw differences. This grassy stretch was larger, and there did not seem to be any watering holes.

"Giddyup," he said, urging his horse to a trot.

The bullet tore his hat from his head. Slocum bent low, sawed at the reins, and turned his horse so he could ride back to where his hat lay on a grassy mound. Bending low in the saddle, he scooped it up. He had money now and could buy another hat, but something else occurred to him.

He did not want the Gila Rangers figuring out who had invaded their territory.

More bullets drove Slocum downhill into a patch of briars. His horse reared and almost threw him. He held his seat and got out of the tangle, going back downhill. His original plan had been to give Tolliver time to escape. If his partner hadn't gotten away by now, he never would. Slocum abandoned the notion of going over the hill and finding the Gila Road on the far side of the mountain.

His new plan was simpler: survive.

"He's goin' that'a way, fellows!" came the cry. "Down toward the valley. Head 'im off!"

Slocum slowed and finally stopped, finding a spot to rest his frightened horse. A slow smile came to his lips when three men pounded past, intent only on reaching the foot of the hill and catching their elusive quarry. If he wanted, Slocum could follow at a more leisurely pace, and they would never see him.

Instead, he turned back uphill. Let the vigilantes chase their tails all over the mountain. He would be long gone by the time they figured out he had not been spooked and herded ahead of them.

Dawn stroked fiery fingers across the dusty eastern sky by the time he got off the mountain and headed for the Butterfield Stagecoach station. He had changed his plans over and over, but the original one seemed to have been the best.

It worked.

The dust storm that blew through the desert forced Slocum to stay at the way station longer than he had anticipated. Still, after all he had been through, he needed the respite. He tended his horse, fed from a table filled with beans, tortillas, and tequila supplied by the Mexican stationmaster's wife, and even slept enough to get rid of the edgy feeling.

"I'm much obliged," Slocum said as the wind died down and the oppressive heat returned.

"You can ride in with the stage," the stationmaster said. "It will be along shortly."

"Butterfield must keep a better schedule than I'd have thought possible. The storm ought to have—"

"Dust, ha!" the stationmaster said, waving his hands about. "It does not stop *our* stage!"

"I'd as soon get into Neutral," Slocum said. "A friend is waiting for me."

"You are welcome to stay longer," the man said with some longing. Slocum knew the money he had paid for the food and bed was outrageous, but he hadn't cared. In a way, the greenbacks were simply being returned to the company where they had been stolen. But he wanted to make sure that Tolliver had made it alive—and had the rest of the loot hidden where they could retrieve it later.

"Thanks but—" Slocum stiffened when he saw a new dust cloud swirling up on the desert. This one came along the road, but it was from Neutral. The stagecoach the stationmaster had mentioned was coming from the other direction, from Los Angeles. To kick up that much dust meant a party of at least three men.

Who would be out on the road in this heat but the law? Or the Gila Rangers.

"José, José," called the man's wife. "It is Mr. Yarrow and his men again."

"Yarrow? You know him?" asked Slocum.

"Why, yes, yes, I do. He comes out once or twice a week."

"Why?"

The stationmaster shrugged. "He likes my wife's food. He and his men eat, they talk, then they ride away again. Always does he pay well, as you did. Do you know him? He is a generous man."

Slocum said nothing. Yarrow had ridden hard and fast and was entering the way station yard. To cut and run now would draw unwanted attention.

"Well, well, if it isn't Mr. Slocum. How are you doing?" said Yarrow.

"Still hunting for a job," Slocum said. "Thought I might find something this side of town."

"Did you?" Yarrow and his men dismounted.

"Not a thing. Not even the mines that are on the other side."

"Fancy that," Yarrow said dryly. "Mines tend to cause boomtowns to spring up like boils on a greenhorn's ass. No mines, no town."

"Just way stations," said the stationmaster. "You want food?"

"And some of that special *pulque*," Yarrow said, grinning. "You tried José's *pulque*, Slocum?"

"Just the tequila." Slocum wanted to ask Yarrow why he rode out—often, from the stationmaster's account. Somehow, the way Yarrow talked kept Slocum from getting out his questions.

"We'll sample some, then go on back to Neutral. That suit you, Slocum?"

Somehow, Slocum got the feeling there wasn't a good alternative to going along with whatever Yarrow wanted.

11

"Buy you a drink, Slocum? The trail's been mighty hot and dusty. More so than usual." Yarrow looked sideways at him, always judging, looking for something. But what? Slocum had ridden with Yarrow and his two partners, and had not figured out what they were doing out on the Gila Road. As far as he could tell, they had simply ridden out to the way station, eaten, drunk some of José's *pulque,* then turned around and returned to Neutral.

It made no sense.

"I'll take a rain check on that."

"Rain? Here?" Yarrow took off his hat and squinted at the cloudless sky. It had been hot all day and was getting hotter. If it rained more than five inches in any single year, people would start talking about building boats.

"People to see, things to do," Slocum said, not happy with the way Yarrow tried to worm information from him.

"Later then," Yarrow said. The two men riding with him had already disappeared, gone into their hidey-holes to do whatever it was they did when they vanished so completely.

Slocum let Yarrow enter the Dead Lizard Dance Hall before riding on to the stables. He had no reason to hide his destination from Yarrow, but it felt right. Slocum saw that Tolliver's horse was already in a stall and had been tended. Slocum spent twenty minutes working on his own horse, rubbing it down and seeing it had ample water and some food before he went to find Tolliver.

The man had money and plenty of it, but Slocum trusted Tolliver not to rush into a saloon and begin spreading around the greenbacks, making a spectacle of himself. Of all the places he might be, Tolliver was most likely at Dr. Martin's office.

Slocum went in, and was pleased to see his guess was right. But his heart jumped into his throat when he caught sight of Tolliver's face.

"What's wrong?" Slocum asked, going to the man's side. Clay Tolliver turned a pale face upward to him and tried to smile. It made him look like a fleshless skull.

"Bad pain, Slocum. Wasn't as ready for a long ride as I thought. Doc's got me doped up with some of his special medicine."

"Cheap whiskey, more 'n likely," Slocum said.

"Harder stuff even than that. Laudanum. Makes me a mite queasy and a whole lot more light-headed."

"Where'd you stash the money?" asked Slocum.

"I ain't gonna die on you, John. Trust me. I've been close before, and this doesn't feel like it. Just so tired. And I hurt. God, how I *hurt*."

"Where?" Slocum demanded.

"My side, where the bullet ripped into me."

"The money," Slocum said impatiently. "Where'd you stash the loot?"

"Stables," Tolliver said, trying to smile. He had known what Slocum had meant and tried to make a joke. It was a feeble one, but showed Tolliver was still his ordinary, ornery self. "In the stall with my horse. Under a pile of fresh manure where nobody'd ever find it by accident."

"Tainted money," Slocum said, but he was talking to a

sleeping man. Tolliver had curled up on a small cot, and slept now. Slocum waited around a spell, until Tolliver's breathing evened out and some color returned to his face.

Slocum went back into the hot noonday sun and wiped sweat from his forehead with a red bandanna. In seconds, it was completely drenched. He had hoped to leave Neutral soon, but from Tolliver's condition, it might take another week for him to recover enough. But they had some of the Gila Rangers' stolen money. That made the wait a little easier—and a little harder.

Walker wasn't the kind of owlhoot to tolerate theft of his money.

Slocum stepped back and tried to press himself through the wall when he spotted Sheriff Hardeen and Walker coming down the middle of Neutral's main street. The set of their shoulders told him the two were determined. But to do what?

Slocum crouched and found a small bit of shade. Not only was it a trifle cooler, but he was out of sight as the two men passed Dr. Martin's office on their way to the bank. Curious, Slocum trailed them. He sucked in his breath when he saw three Gila Rangers outside the bank.

He doubted Walker intended robbing the bank with Hardeen at his shoulder, but Slocum had seen stranger things. The vigilantes paid the sheriff some deference, but when their boss and Hardeen went inside, they shared some joke at the lawman's expense and went back to studying the bank exterior.

As if they were thinking on robbing it. Again.

Slocum wondered what business Walker and Hardeen had with Matthew Reilly, but he had no way of getting into the bank to find out. The thick adobe walls prevented even a hint of sound from escaping. More than this, the Gila Rangers patrolling outside would stop him from snooping.

He didn't want to be too conspicuous, not after stealing

Walker's loot, but curiosity was getting the better of him. What business did the sheriff have with Matthew Reilly? And with Walker along?

Slocum found he didn't have to go spying. Reilly and the other two came out. Hardeen spoke to them a few more minutes, shook the new banker's meaty paw of a hand, then sauntered off, as if he did not have a care in the world. Slocum waited to see where Reilly and Walker went.

The two went around to the back of the bank to palaver. Slocum saw his chance when the three Gila Rangers were sent off. They headed for the nearest saloon, and Slocum headed for the bank roof. Wood beams jutted out of the sides of the wall, supporting the roof. He jumped, grabbed, and pulled himself up to the thatched roof. For the first time Slocum realized how vulnerable this bank was. Chopping through the roof would take less than a minute.

Once in the back room with the ponderous vault, a bank robber could blow the safe with a case of dynamite, if even that much were needed.

Slocum pushed aside his thoughts of robbing the bank when he heard Walker and Matthew Reilly in back. He flopped to his belly and inched forward so he could peer over the edge of the roof. The two men stood almost nose-to-nose, arguing.

"You can't take that much!" protested Reilly. "It's out of the question. Why, it's *robbery*!"

"That ever stopped you before, banker man?"

"Don't speak to me in that tone," Reilly said, his Irish temper building.

"Truth hurts, don't it?" Walker was pleased with himself. Slocum saw it in the way the man stood, chin thrust out in a pose just begging for someone to clip him on the jaw.

"Our dealings are past, Walker."

"You got that wrong. They are just startin', Reilly. First thing is for you to tell me when you can get a pile of money into the bank."

"My mistakes are just that, mistakes. We're finished, done, over."

"And here I wanted to take out . . . a loan." Walker laughed harshly, shoved Reilly back, and pushed past him. Matthew Reilly sputtered, then hurried after the self-styled vigilante.

Slocum had no idea what it was all about, but by the time the men stepped out into the street in front of the bank, they had both cooled down and looked downright friendly. That set Slocum to thinking. He waited for them to head for the same saloon where the three men from Walker's gang had already gone before he dropped to the ground.

He dusted himself off, then started the long walk up the hill toward Grace's house. He needed some information, and she was the only one likely to give it to him. Knocking on the door, he waited, wondering if she was even home. If she had any sense, she would have jumped onto the first Butterfield stage leaving Neutral and left this one-horse town for good.

The door opened. For a moment, it was as if she did not recognize him. Then Grace's face lit up like the noonday sun, and she had her arms around his neck. The kiss proved she knew exactly who he was.

"John, I thought you had left!"

"Can't leave, not yet," he said, remembering the way he had mentally wrestled with what to tell Grace—and whether to ask her to ride along when he did leave Neutral. With the money Tolliver had stashed in the stable, they could do well for quite a while.

Somewhere else. Anywhere else.

"Come in. Don't stand out there in the heat." She ushered him into the front room. It was hardly cooler there, but Slocum was glad for the pitcher of water Grace had on the table. He drank two glasses and considered a third before deciding that was rude.

"Where have you been?" she asked.

"Poking around, maybe where I shouldn't look."

"What are you saying?" She sat beside him on the small settee, her leg pressing against his. Slocum found it harder to think when Grace was this close.

"I wanted to ask about the bank and your uncle."

"Business," Grace said, sighing deeply. He couldn't help noticing the way her breasts rose and fell under the crisp white blouse. In deference to the heat, she wore nothing under the linen. Slocum saw how Grace's nipples hardened and pressed into the fabric, telling him where her thoughts were.

Too.

"Later," he said, turning a little. His arms went around her. It felt like the most natural thing in the world. She pressed against him, and their mouths met. The kiss was soft and tender at the start, but it grew in passion and intensity. Her tongue flicked out against Slocum's lips, then boldly plunged into his mouth. His own dueled with hers until they were gasping for breath.

Grace's fingers worked on his shirt and gunbelt and jeans, fluttering lightly here and there on his naked flesh for several minutes while they kissed. Somehow, she managed to get his clothes off. He kicked off his boots while she unbuttoned her blouse and let her snowy white melons swing free.

Slocum took a deep breath. He got hard just looking at those luscious mounds. He buried his face between them, kissing and licking. Then he worked his own magic getting her free of her skirt. Grace dropped to her knees in front of him, then bent over.

He gasped as she took him in her mouth. Her eager tongue found new places to stimulate him. Deep inside his loins it felt as if a runaway ore cart was rumbling down the tracks, about to crash spectacularly. He fought to keep himself under control as she licked up and down his hardening length. After a few minutes, he could take no more of it.

"You're too good. I'm going to explode if you use your mouth on me anymore," he said.

She stood in front of him, cupped her own breasts, and squeezed down hard on the cherry-colored nipples. Grace widened her stance slightly, exposing the fleecy triangle of bright red between her milky thighs. She stepped forward and climbed onto the settee, her knees on either side of Slocum's thighs.

Lowering herself slowly, Grace wiggled her rump and positioned her nether lips directly over the tip where her mouth had been seconds before.

Slocum stroked along her sleek sides, then reached behind and cupped her fleshy buttocks. Kneading them like mounds of dough, he pulled her toward him and let her settle down. They gasped in unison as he slid swiftly up into her well-oiled female sheath. Grace paused, then began rolling her hips, stirring his manhood about in her most intimate realm like a spoon in a mixing bowl.

"You're so tight around me," Slocum got out. "And hot. So hot."

Sweat poured in rivers down his face.

"Feels like I got me a red-hot poker inside," Grace said, bending forward to kiss and lick and nip at his earlobes. "And it excites me so!"

She rocked forward, then back, driving his fleshy spike in and out of her tightness. Slowly at first, the woman built up speed until the settee creaked under the strain. She rose, then slammed down hard onto his length. He ground his hips around to give them both even more pleasure.

Not one to be passive, Slocum again grabbed handfuls

of firm ass cheeks and began lifting and dropping Grace in the rhythm that pleased him most. But he soon began to lose control. She gasped and moaned and her hips flew like shuttlecocks. Slocum applied even more pressure to her rump, and began heaving himself upward to meet her every plunge down.

Deep inside him, it felt as if she had lit a fuse leading to a powder keg buried in his balls. The fuse sizzled and hissed and burned faster. When Grace gasped and threw her head back, red hair flying about her face like some colorful cloud, every muscle inside her tensed.

This clamped down so hard on Slocum, he exploded. He stretched his legs straight in front of him and pulled her down with all his strength. Their bodies ground together in an erotic release that was over far too soon for both of them.

"So intense," Grace sighed, pushing strands of her coppery hair from her eyes. She grinned, and it was no innocent smile. "Might be we can make it last longer upstairs in my bed."

"Might be," Slocum agreed. The naked woman pushed away and dashed up the stairs. Slocum enjoyed the sights following her up, but not as much as the protracted lovemaking that ensued. Sated and tired, they lay in the bed until Slocum noticed the sun had gone down.

He sat bolt upright.

"What's wrong, John?"

"The reason I came up here."

"Business," she sighed, stroking his leg and working over a bit farther. "Monkey business."

"Bank business," he said. He caught her slender wrist and kept her hand from trying to find any life left at all in his dormant organ. "What business dealings has your uncle had with Walker?"

"Walker? Why, none that I know of. Uncle Matthew has been out in California for the past few years. He might have known Walker there, but I can't say."

"I think the two are up to something crooked."

"What?" This got Grace's attention. "Something at the bank?"

"Could be. I've got this notion your uncle is financing the Gila Rangers to rob the stagecoaches and maybe even the bank when your pa still ran it."

"That'd mean Uncle Matthew indirectly killed my father! That's a terrible thing to say. They are—were—brothers!"

"There's no denying Walker and Reilly know each other." Slocum related what he had overheard, not telling Grace where he had been during the spying.

"Bankers know all kinds of people, and not only the law-abiding ones. I'm not so sure you don't have a grudge against Walker, John. He seems to have the best interests of Neutral at heart. And Sheriff Hardeen has done nothing to stop him. In fact, he even rides with the Gila Rangers at times."

"I know. I think the sheriff might be involved too. There's a powerful lot of money involved." Slocum held off telling Grace about the money he and Tolliver had stolen from Walker's camp. It would only muddy the waters.

"What do you think is going to happen?" She sat up, pulling the bedclothes up chastely to her neck. This suited Slocum fine. Otherwise, he found it hard to think straight.

"Walker and the Gila Rangers are going to rob the bank again. Might be this time they'll do it when no one's around."

"Like now? Tonight?"

"Is there anything special locked in the vault?"

For a moment, Grace did not answer. Slocum turned and saw the woman's expression.

"I was right," he said. "There's something worth robbing locked up there."

"Gold, gold from three of the mines. The owners have been hoarding it, and pooled it so they could ship it out all at once on the stage. By going in together, they can hire an extra guard to protect it."

"An extra guard's not going to mean squat if the gold is snatched from the bank before shipment," Slocum said. He swung his feet over the side of the bed and padded quickly downstairs to get dressed.

"What are you going to do, John?" Grace trailed him. She began fumbling on her own clothing. "You can't leave me out. I own the bank. Uncle Matthew is only running it for me."

"There won't be a dime left in the bank if this gold is stolen," Slocum said. "Every mattress in the county will be lumpy with gold and crinkly with greenbacks before the miners put anything into a bank with the reputation of being robbed over and over."

"I'll be ruined," Grace said, anger growing. "How could Uncle Matthew permit such a thing to happen? I can't believe it of him. I just can't."

Slocum strapped on his gunbelt and pulled on his boots. Grace might not be able to think poorly of her uncle, but Slocum was not so sure of the man's honesty. They had gotten off on the wrong foot, but seeing Reilly with Walker cemented the notion the banker was crooked.

Knowing he could do nothing to prevent it, Slocum allowed Grace to accompany him to the bank. It might be a long, lonely vigil—or it might prove to be hotter than hell. Either way, she had a right to know about her uncle and his intentions.

12

"We should hide in the bank and catch them if they try to break in," Grace said, warming to her novel idea. "We must protect the gold awaiting shipment at all costs." She was pleased with herself for having hit on such a decisive course of action.

"It would be at all costs," Slocum said acidly. "We'd pay with our lives doing it that way."

"So do you have a better idea?" Grace sounded snappish at having her fine idea criticized. Slocum did not blame her for the way she reacted, but she knew nothing of laying a trap or how to stay alive when the lead started flying. The Gila Rangers would break into the bank and be on edge, ready to shoot anything that moved. That was precisely the wrong time to go after them.

It might be better to let them plunder the bank vault, *then* stop them. They would feel good about their easy victory, and their guard would drop. That was definitely a better time to stop them. And, Slocum had to admit, it might be a good time to take the gold from them for himself.

He glanced at Grace, and the idea evaporated like water spilled on a hot griddle. There was a moment of sizzle, then it vanished in a billow of steam. She had little enough legacy left by her father. To destroy the bank and the miners' confidence in it would only accelerate the death of Neutral as a town.

Still, Slocum saw how the town was dying on the vine. It was only a matter of time before the mines petered out and the miners turned back into prospectors in some other boomtown, those miners that had an inclination. Others would hunt for different mining operations, and there were none in the area. Tombstone had petered out. Word of copper to the east and south ran rampant, but that was not the way to get rich.

Gold. Silver. Those were metals worth risking your life for. Even better, they were metals worth risking someone else's life for.

"We ought to check on Clay and see how he is getting along," Grace said, her mood changing mercurially. "He was so sick when he got back. What was it you two did out in the desert? Jeopardizing his life was a terrible thing to do, John."

He shook his head. How she got from protecting the gold in her bank to how poorly Tolliver felt confused him.

"Might be best if you went on over to Dr. Martin's office and waited there," Slocum suggested. "I can watch the bank from over yonder, in the shadows by the bookstore."

"You can see anyone coming or going from there," Grace said, judging angles and distances. "Could you do anything to *stop* a robbery if you are alone? There would be several of them and only one of you."

"One of me along with six tried and true friends," Slocum said, drawing his six-shooter and holding it out for her to see. "Any ruckus I cause is likely to bring folks running."

"Well, all right. Clay does need tending, and I'm not sure I'd be any good if fighting started. I am simply too involved. And I cannot believe Uncle Matthew knows anything about a robbery of the bank."

"For your sake, I hope you're right. Get on along. If nothing happens before dawn, I'll mosey over to the surgery and let you know how boring it has been all night."

"Very well," Grace said. She stood on tiptoe and gave him a quick kiss on the lips, a wine-sweet reminder of how they had spent the afternoon. Then the redhead hurried off, muttering to herself. Slocum tried to decipher her words about Clay Tolliver, but they were too low to catch.

He shrugged it off as he pressed his back against the wooden wall and vanished into shadow. From there he could see both the bank's front door and the side. With a little imagination he could picture what went on behind the bank also. Slocum sat in the dirt and waited. During the war he had been a sniper and had spent long hours doing nothing but watching and waiting. It stood him in good stead now. He might be out all night long.

It turned out he had less than an hour to wait. The sun had sunk below the horizon three hours earlier, and the darkness in Neutral was punctuated only by sputtering gaslights in front of the saloons. Riding slowly, making very little noise, came four masked men from the west—from the direction of the Gila Rangers' camp. They dismounted at the side of the bank where Slocum could see what they were up to.

He had hit on the idea of entering the bank by chopping through the thatched roof. Two of the robbers had the same idea. With axes, they clambered to the roof, walked off a measured distance that put them directly over the back roof, then began chopping.

Slocum jumped when sparks flew up from one robber's ax. His hand had gone instinctively to his six-shooter at the sound of metal grating on metal. It took him a few seconds to figure out what the robbers had just discovered.

One called down, "Damned iron bars. All through the roof. We can't chop them with no ax."

"Get on down then," ordered the leader. Slocum recognized the voice. Walker's sidekick named Slim was in charge of the robbers tonight. The four circled the bank, then went to the front door, where they held a small conference, huddled in a tight ring.

Slocum heard part of the argument, then it became a moot point. Slim stepped back and pointed at the front doors. The two men with axes went after the doors as if their lives depended on it. The staccato chopping sounds carried through the streets of Neutral loud enough to wake the dead.

No one took notice, not even the sheriff. Especially Sheriff Hardeen, Slocum decided.

The doors came unhinged under the onslaught and fell inward. Where there had been frantic chopping one instant, now there was only silence. The ruckus from all the saloons had hidden the noisy entry into the bank.

Slocum moved around to get a view of what went on inside the darkened bank. One robber lit a lucifer, then swore when he burned his fingers as it hissed and popped down to a nubbin. Slim got a lantern from somewhere inside the bank. A second lucifer ignited the wick.

Slocum wondered what he ought to do now. Let the robbers open the vault and catch them red-handed? Stop the robbery before they got the vault open? Preventing robberies was something new for Slocum, and he had to think about it.

That hesitation saved his life. He was still across the street near the bookstore when the guts of the bank erupted in flame. The explosion shook the ground and knocked him off his feet. Slocum sat down hard, clutching his Colt Navy to be sure he didn't lose it. Shaken, he got to his feet and saw the tongues of flame licking out the front door.

"What did you fools do?" he wondered aloud. Slocum started for the bank, then stopped when he heard the thunder of hooves coming in his direction. Walker rode at the front of a band of the vigilantes, looking madder than a wet hen. The Gila Ranger hit the ground running and pushed past Slocum.

Then Walker dug in his heels and spun around.

"What the hell'd you do?"

"I didn't do anything," Slocum said. "I was across the street when the bank blew up."

"What?" Walker's eyes went big. "They didn't have any—" He bit off whatever else he had to say, but Slocum finished the sentence for him. Slim and the other three robbers hadn't brought along any dynamite on their robbery.

So why did the bank explode?

"What's goin' on?" demanded Sheriff Hardeen, pushing through the rapidly forming crowd. "Get back. There's nothin' to see here."

"Put the danged fire out, Sheriff," someone in the crowd called. "The whole town'll burn to a cinder if you don't do something about that fire."

"Yes, right, get a bucket brigade going. Use the water in the horse troughs. Someone back there in the crowd, get water barrels and make sure we're supplied." The sheriff knew what to do, but was confused that he had to do it. He decided to pursue a course more in line with his usual duties.

Hardeen turned on Slocum as Walker had.

"What are you doing here? You responsible?"

"Like I told Walker, I was passing by when the bank blew up. It's a mystery to me." Slocum did not have to feign innocence. He had no idea what had happened. He stood and watched the bucket brigade begin moving tiny amounts of water from down the street to the bank. The fire burned itself out sooner than the men could have put it out, but they still declared victory over the evils fire could do and went off to get ripsnorting drunk to celebrate.

"The inside of the bank is a mess," opined one of Walker's Gila Rangers. The man gagged and hustled out. "They got burned to death inside. All four of them."

From the man's brief excursion into the bank, he could not have known only four men had died—unless it had been the plan that only four would rob the bank. Hardeen took no notice of the slip, and Slocum wasn't going to point it out. He decided it would do no good.

He pulled up his bandanna and started poking in the charred remains of the bank lobby. The mask of the robber nearest the door had been burned away, leaving his face almost untouched by blast or flame.

"You ever see this one before, Sheriff?" asked Slocum as he pointed to Slim's body. The other three were burned beyond recognition, but Slim had somehow survived total disfigurement, for all the good it did. He was as dead as the others.

"Never seen him before," Hardeen said, barely glancing at the body. "What the devil happened? Did they break in, try to blow the safe with dynamite, and somehow got caught in their own explosion?"

"Doesn't look that way, Sheriff," Slocum said, stepping through the rubble. The safe was almost pristine. Some smoke from the fire had darkened it, but otherwise it had escaped without more than a scratch or two. Slocum began looking around, and saw how the entire wall between the lobby and the back room where the safe stood had been blasted away.

Something had been placed on the outside of the wall. When it blew, the force of the blast went outward through the lobby, leaving the back room unscathed. Some of the thatching in the ceiling had caught fire and one viga smoldered, but Slocum saw that the crisscrossing iron rods in the ceiling were still intact.

The bank had been built to withstand just about any robbery, but that did not explain the source of the explosion.

"You, Reilly," shouted Sheriff Hardeen. "Get in here. What happened?"

"It looks as if I caught some robbers at work, that's what happened, you harebrained fool!" raged Matthew Reilly. He glared at Walker, as if challenging him to speak. Walker put his hand on the butt of his six-gun in its cross-draw holster, but said nothing.

"Explain yourself," said Hardeen.

"I booby-trapped the bank, that's what I did. I feared there would be a robbery attempt, and I wanted to make sure it was not successful!"

"You done killed four men," Hardeen pointed out.

"Four bank robbers killed themselves. If they hadn't been intent on stealing the contents of my vault, they wouldn't have stumbled on the trip wire."

"Don't rightly know how to go on this one. Putting a dynamite trap in your bank like this was mighty dangerous."

"Only to robbers. I saved the county the cost of getting a judge here from Prescott and trying those owlhoots," said Matthew Reilly. "As if you'd ever have caught them." Again he glared at Walker, challenging the vigilante to say anything.

Slocum had wondered if Reilly had somehow backed the Gila Rangers in their robberies, but it was clear there was nothing but bad blood between him and Walker. When Walker had promised to rob the bank, taking the bank's good name along with a passel of gold, Reilly had defended the bank the best way he could.

The two men weren't in cahoots. If anything, they were mortal enemies.

"You recognize any of the robbers?" Slocum asked Reilly.

"Don't go steppin' on my toes, Slocum," snapped Hardeen. "I ask the questions. I'm the sheriff in these parts."

Hardeen glanced down at Slim and paused. Slocum knew the lawman recognized Slim as one of the Gila Rangers but would say nothing about it. Whether he got a cut of everything Walker stole or was just scared spitless hardly mattered. He'd failed to ask the questions he should have, had he been honest.

"Get these . . . smelly gents over to the undertaker's parlor pronto," he said. He waved two of the Gila Rangers to the task, but they waited until Walker gave them the go-ahead. They gingerly moved the charred bodies.

"Yes, get those owlhoots out of my bank," said Reilly. "I need to get a carpenter in as soon as I can to rebuild. We will *not* miss a day of service to Neutral!"

"Fine words, Mr. Reilly," said Walker, "but you got a definite problem right now. Without doors—or much in the way of a wall or ceiling—any thief can walk right on up and steal the gold in your safe. In the name of the Gila Rangers, I'll be stationing a half dozen of my men to guard the safe."

"You seem to know what's in the vault, sir," Reilly said coldly. "You are personally responsible for protecting the assets of this bank until I can get the building repaired."

"That's fine by me," Walker said. "We formed the Gila Rangers for duty such as this, didn't we, Sheriff?"

"Uh, yes, of course. I can post a deputy here also." Hardeen sounded tentative, unsure of himself or his duty. It might have been the first time he had thought like a lawman in months.

"No need, Sheriff," Walker said coldly, glaring at Hardeen. Slocum watched as the lawman wilted like a daisy in the hot sun. "You run along now, and see to keepin' the peace in the rest of town. Me and the boys can take care of Mr. Reilly's bank."

Matthew Reilly hesitated, then said, "I'll keep you company, Walker. After all, there's no reason you should put yourselves out on my account. This isn't *your* bank."

The battle of wills went on, but Slocum stepped away from the burned interior of the adobe bank. He doubted Walker would try to steal the gold now, not with everyone in town knowing he had vowed to protect it against any more robbers.

And if the Gila Rangers did pry open the vault and steal the gold under Reilly's nose, it didn't matter to Slocum. He knew where they would take their loot once they left Neutral. And he would be there to steal it from them again, just as he and Tolliver had taken that mail sack stuffed with greenbacks.

Slocum went off whistling, ready to down a drink or two, then go to Dr. Martin's surgery and let Grace know what had happened.

He felt eyes on him as he went up the creaking wood steps leading into the Sundog Saloon. Slocum glanced over his shoulder and saw Yarrow watching him like a coyote eyes a slow rabbit.

13

Slocum felt alone in the crowded saloon. All around, men congratulated themselves on putting out the fire, even if they had nothing to do with the actual work of hauling water or standing near the blistering heat to put out the flames. He sipped at his whiskey, thinking of the money he'd used to pay for it.

Stolen.

If Walker and his Gila Rangers had not robbed the stagecoach, Slocum would not have had any money at all. In a way, it was too bad the Gila Rangers had failed to rob the bank, its vault bulging with gold and gold dust from several mines. Slocum did not care about the bank's reputation—or Grace's ownership of it—as much as he did about getting enough money to move on.

He and Tolliver were owed.

But where did Grace come into it? He shook his head, knocked back the drink, and signaled the barkeep for another. Robbing the bank was robbing her. She owned it, even if she could not run it. From the way her uncle acted, she might not be legal owner long because he would do her out of it somehow. Matthew Reilly seemed to Slocum to be as much of a crook as Walker.

Then there was the peculiar confrontation Slocum had overheard. Reilly and Walker knew each other from some prior dealing, but now were on opposite sides. Walker had tried to steal what Reilly had locked up in the vault. How long before Reilly decided to throw in with the outlaw? Would he ever? Grace might be out a passel of money in a hurry if her uncle turned against her.

The man's violent temper told Slocum that that might happen at any instant.

He finished another drink, turned, and leaned his elbows on the bar as he looked around. Miners from all over the countryside had flocked to town, to celebrate the new strike by socializing and drinking. A fight started in one corner of the Sundog. Slocum saw how the others put down bets. Usually, he would join in, taking odds, angling to remove a few dollars from drunken miners more interested in a good time than winning.

He felt curiously hollow now. Something was lacking— or he was missing something. That bothered him more than anything else. He had missed something obvious.

Leaving the saloon, he stepped back into the chilly night. Slocum expected to spot Yarrow across the street watching for him. The stylishly dressed man was nowhere to be seen, and his partners always vanished like whiskey on the house whenever they set foot in town.

"It's Yarrow that's spooking me," Slocum muttered to himself, but that didn't feel right. He'd missed some other detail. It began working into his brain like a burr under a saddle blanket. Shrugging it off, Slocum went directly for Dr. Martin's office. A single light burned inside, showing Grace was still there with Tolliver, as he had suggested. She was always amenable to visiting his partner, and Slocum knew it had kept her out of the tornado of trouble that had swept through Neutral earlier.

Slocum turned the doorknob into the surgery, but it was

locked. He rattled it, to make sure, then knocked on the door and called, "It's me. Slocum."

Almost a minute later, the door was unlocked and opened a fraction of an inch. Slocum recognized Grace's bright emerald eyes staring at him. She stepped back and let him in.

"Are you all right?" he asked, wondering at the length of time it had taken for her to get to the door and open it.

"Oh, I'm fine." She looked over her shoulder in Tolliver's direction. The man lay in the middle of a rumpled bed, snoring loudly.

"What about him?"

"Oh, he's fine too," she said, averting her eyes.

"You hear about the bank?"

"Dr. Martin stopped by right after it blew up to tell me what happened. Then he went to celebrate."

"Figures," Slocum said. The doctor had not bothered to stop by to see if anyone was injured. He had gone directly for the nearest saloon to knock back a few more ounces of rotgut.

"The Gila Rangers are guarding the safe?" she asked, worried.

"It'll be sunup soon, and they won't be able to crack the safe in broad daylight without everyone in town seeing," Slocum said. "The vault is as secure as if your uncle sat on it personally." Slocum did not share with Grace his thoughts on how secure that might be.

"What are we going to do?"

Slocum looked at the sleeping Tolliver. The man had recovered fast, and would be up to leaving Neutral in another day or two. They had simply pushed his strength to the limit too soon.

"The Gila Rangers need to be brought to justice," Slocum said, "but Hardeen is in with them. If he isn't, he is a dupe, and that might be even worse."

"We can't arrest them ourselves," Grace said. "And I know I can't keep the bank going much longer. Rebuilding is going to cost too much, if the devastation is anywhere near as bad as Dr. Martin said."

"Your uncle booby-trapped it, so he's responsible for the destruction."

"I want to see, John. Please."

Grace seemed in a powerful hurry to leave. Slocum wondered if Tolliver had taken a turn for the worse while she was there and it was beginning to wear on her. Slocum escorted her from the doctor's office to the bank. He went cold inside when he neared the chopped-down doors leading into the burned-out lobby.

"Wait here," he said. "Walker said he was staying."

"But there's no one here!" cried Grace, her hand going to her mouth. "Uncle Matthew!"

Slocum stepped over fallen vigas and prowled the lobby, then went to the back room where the safe stood. Grace came up behind him, putting her hand on his shoulder.

"They stole the gold!" she exclaimed.

"Doesn't look as if Walker is making any excuses now."

"We've got to get it back, John. Please. I don't know what I'm going to do. This will ruin me! And it besmirches my father's honor."

Slocum had never liked her father. Besides, dead men worried less about honor and more about other things, like maggots and dirt in the face. He did not burden her with his thoughts on that. Instead, he saw a chance for him and Tolliver—and maybe, Grace, if she had a streak of larceny in her—to come out of this ahead.

He and Tolliver had already stolen Walker's scrip. Recovering the gold the Gila Rangers had taken from the bank vault and keeping it would solve a lot of his problems. They had considered robbing the bank and had thwarted Walker's men before. It was time to finish what he and Tolliver had started before his partner took a bullet to the chest.

"I'll get it, Grace," he said, wondering if he ought to tell her he intended keeping anything he took from the Gila Rangers. Her lovely face looked so angelic, so lovely and trusting, he held back.

"I'm going with you," she said. "No, John, don't argue. It's my bank, my responsibility. You said yourself Sheriff Hardeen was in Walker's hip pocket. Who else is there? A federal marshal has no jurisdiction over just a bank robbery."

"Even if a marshal got interested, a federal marshal'd be a hundred miles or more away," Slocum said. "But it'll be dangerous, Grace. Walker is a killer." He remembered how Utah Jaeger had been double-crossed and murdered while Walker laughed.

"There's nothing left for me in Neutral. Let's recover the gold."

Slocum decided it was not the right time to mention simply collecting Tolliver after they stole back the gold and riding off. He was not sure when the time would be right, but Grace was so fired up now she would never agree to keeping the gold for herself.

After she saw how vicious Walker really was, she might change her opinion.

"Get into riding gear," Slocum told her. "I'll saddle Tolliver's horse for you and be up at your house in a half hour."

"Very well, John. And thank you for understanding." Again she gave him the delicious, lingering kiss on the lips. Then Grace hurried off. If he had any intention of digging in the manure pile in the stable and riding off with the greenbacks they had already recovered, that kiss kept him from doing it.

"The gold," he told himself. "With the gold we'll have more choices."

"It's getting mighty hot," Grace said, using a damp handkerchief to mop at her brow. Her nose had gotten sunburned in spite of the wide-brimmed hat she'd pulled down low. "And my eyes are watering from squinting all the time."

"It's bright and hot," he agreed. They had ridden only an hour. The real heat would come in a few hours. By then Slocum intended to be into the mountains, where it was cooler and pools of water provided ample amounts of the most important necessity of life in the desert. "You want to rest a spell?"

"No, let's keep going. It will be cooler, won't it? Up there?" She pointed up the winding, rocky trail into the hills where Walker had his camp.

"Yep," was all Slocum said. He dismounted and walked, giving his horse a chance to rest. They had made good time, all things considered, but he wanted to find Walker's trail and reassure himself he'd headed in the right direction. The rocky terrain and shifting sand had prevented him from finding any trace of the Gila Rangers. That meant he had to push on to the camp and hope Walker was still there.

With the stolen gold.

"We should have brought a spare horse," he said, realizing the gold would weigh down his mount too much when they tried to get away. Slocum wondered if he could steal a couple of horses from Walker's remuda. How much was too much to expect? He had learned to keep his plans simple because less went wrong.

"I want to go on, John, but I'm so tired I can hardly stay in the saddle."

"Rest," he said. "In a few minutes we'll be at a watering hole. Can you last that long?"

"If I have to, I will. I'm sorry about slowing you. It was foolish of me to insist on coming along."

Slocum considered asking how badly she wanted to keep the bank and her father's honor intact. Grace might well damn both her own honor and her father's in exchange for the gold stolen from the vault.

"There," she said, interrupting his train of thought. "There's the watering hole." Her horse reared, forcing her to fight to keep it under control. Slocum turned, grabbed the reins, and dragged down until the horse quieted. He led the way to the watering hole, where the two horses greedily sucked in water.

"Pull your horse back in a few minutes so it won't bloat," he said.

"I don't know how to thank you for all you've done," she said. "And all you're doing. Nothing is as important to me as making a success of the bank. It's all my father left me."

"Memories," Slocum said, "don't buy victuals. The bank is going to be a memory sooner or later. Neutral is dying and will blow away like dust in the wind when the mines peter out."

"I know, I know," she said, tugging at her horse's reins to get it away from the water. "But I have to try. Giving up isn't in me, John."

"I understand," he said. He appreciated persistence. It made the decisions coming up harder for him, but he had to approve of her desire to make a success of the bank.

Slocum circled the watering hole, looking for any sign of the Gila Rangers. Not even fresh horse dung hinted they had ridden this way. Had Walker pulled up stakes and left Arizona Territory with the gold?

"We have to be more careful from now on," Slocum said. "The Gila Rangers' camp is about ten miles along this trail, and they will have guards posted."

"Should we cut across country?"

Slocum shook his head. Better to be cautious and keep an eye out for sentries. They rode in silence. Slocum strained every sense to find the vigilantes before they found him. Only normal sounds reached his ears. Sniffing the wind brought Apache pine and pinyon, but no campfire. The animals were those that lived on the mountainside. And everything he saw told him that the Gila Rangers had moved on.

"I'll scout on foot from here," Slocum said about a mile from the vigilante camp. "Stay with the horses. Be ready for a quick retreat, if I stir up a hornet's nest."

"I want to be with you," Grace said.

Slocum tethered the horses and motioned for her to follow. He walked slowly, listening for guards as well as how Grace moved. She was not Apache-quiet, but she was good enough. Slocum felt better as he advanced on the camp.

"Well, damn," he said, taking off his hat and wiping sweat from his forehead. Slocum pushed through the undergrowth and into the deserted camp. Fires were long dead. The crude rope corral where the Gila Rangers had tied their horses was empty. The piles of goods around the camp turned out to be empty airtights and other debris from a dozen men who didn't care about sanitation.

"They're gone. Will they be back?" asked Grace, looking around.

"This place is empty and has been for some time," he said. Slocum knew Walker might not have returned when he discovered the theft of the Butterfield loot. Slocum had spooked the vigilantes. Too early. If he had bided his time, he could have stolen the bag stuffed with greenbacks as well as the gold from the bank.

Now? Nothing.

"Where do you think they went, John?"

"Somewhere else," he said, stating the obvious. "Might have hightailed it out of the territory."

"There was a lot of gold in the vault, but would it be enough?" she asked. The red-haired woman chewed her lower lip. "They are greedy, aren't they?"

"There's a lot of that going around," he admitted.

"Walker would stay close, hoping to steal more. And with Hardeen going along with anything he said, they might talk their way out of stealing the gold from the bank."

"So?"

"They have another camp," she said.

"I never saw their trail," Slocum said. "Finding them in these mountains might take weeks. Longer, unless we got lucky."

"I heard Walker mention Esqueleto Mesa once when he was talking with the lieutenant."

"Slim?"

"Yes, yes, that one!" Grace cried. "I remember now because *esqueleto* means skeleton or someone who is really thin, and Slim asked if the place had been named after him."

"Where's this Esqueleto Mesa?" asked Slocum.

"You can almost see it from here. Not more than another five or six miles."

"Can you get there without taking the trail we followed?"

Grace shrugged.

Slocum decided the mountains were so threaded with trails that Walker could get to Esqueleto Mesa in any of a dozen other ways, avoiding the old—and discovered—campground.

"Time's a wasting," Slocum said. Grace hurried to join him as he returned to their horses. They mounted, and Slocum worked out the best way of reaching the mesa poking out from around the side of the mountain where they had missed finding the Gila Rangers.

"What are we going to do when we find them?" Grace asked.

"Get back the gold," he said. Slocum still had no idea what would happen then. Return it to Neutral so Matthew Reilly could do Grace out of her legacy? Keep it so he and Tolliver could live it up? Invite Grace along? Too many questions, not enough answers.

"That's going to be hard, isn't it?"

"Walker isn't the kind of man to hand over something he's stolen," Slocum said. "I sneak into camp, get the gold, then run like a scalded dog. That's the plan."

"You make it sound so . . . cowardly."

Slocum had no answer. It was, but he lacked the firepower and backup to take on the entire band of vigilantes. He frowned when he realized how he had fallen into the trap of thinking of Walker and the Gila Rangers as vigilantes. They were outlaws. They were killers and robbers, and only used the pretense of being vigilantes to kill and steal even more.

"We might consider something else, John. After you get the gold," Grace said. Slocum wondered if she had solved his dilemma for him and was going to suggest they keep the gold for themselves.

He never found out. A bullet whined through the air inches from his head. Slocum jerked around and bent low, grabbing for his rifle. Another slug left a bloody gash along his upper arm. The force of the passing lead took him out of the saddle. His horse bolted, leaving him on the ground with nothing but his Colt Navy against a sniper with a rifle.

"Get away!" he called to Grace, but she was in no position to do anything he asked. The redhead fought to keep from being thrown off her spooked horse.

He whipped out his six-shooter and got off a couple of fast shots intended to drive back the sniper and give Slocum a chance to recover his wits. Slocum could not even see where the rifleman hid. He dropped to his knees and waited for the sniper to show himself.

Sounds came to Slocum from ahead, too many sounds for there to be only one gunman. He saw Grace had regained control of her horse and was heading back down the trail. That was good. It got her out of the line of fire.

It also left Slocum stranded. His horse had run off, and all he had left were four rounds.

Against at least that many Gila Rangers.

He set his jaw and hunted for a place to make what might be his last stand.

14

John Slocum slipped and slid along a short slope covered with loose stones, kicked around, and lay belly-down so he could rest his six-shooter on a rock. He waited for the Gila Rangers to come after him. They hesitated, which gave him a chance to get his breath back. His heart rate slowed, and he was ready for killing.

Death came fast.

Three of the self-styled vigilantes came over the rise at the same time. They foolishly crowded together, as if they thought this would protect them. It did the reverse. Slocum concentrated his fire on the middle man. If he missed one, he might hit one on either side. His first slug brought down the Gila Ranger, who screamed in pain and grabbed his leg, crying for his partners to help. They foolishly turned in confusion to see what was wrong.

Slocum killed the one on the right with a shot to the side of the man's head. He swung to the other man and fired, missing. Realigning his six-shooter, he got the proper sight picture, notches on either side of the blade at the end of his barrel, and squeezed. His Colt Navy clicked loudly on an empty chamber. Out of ammo!

Slocum shoved his six-shooter back into his holster. He

might flee. He might attack. Slocum reacted instinctively. He reached for his broad-bladed knife sheathed at his belt in the small of his back, swarmed upslope, and rushed the remaining man.

The vigilante saw danger coming and lifted his rifle. A shot rang out, but Slocum did not feel the hot lead cutting through his body. Then he crashed into the man and drove him to the ground. Slocum jerked his knife up and started to slash his victim's throat.

The man was dead.

Slocum rolled to the side and avoided the wounded man's wild shots.

"You son of a bitch! You killed Ben and Jerry!" the man screeched. He fired at Slocum, the slugs ripping through the air on either side of his body, going high over Slocum's head.

Slocum balanced his knife, judged the distance, and let it fly. Slocum felt no triumph when the heavy knife sank hilt-deep in the man's throat. He had not aimed for the soft tissue there. He had tried for the man's belly.

Rolling, Slocum scooped up a fallen rifle, then gathered other weapons. He wiped his knife off on the dead man's shirt, resheathed it, and looked around for a way out.

He seemed to have flopped from the frying pan into the fire. No fewer than a half-dozen Gila Rangers opened up on him, driving him back downhill. Slocum fired over his shoulder, but did nothing to stop the pursuit. Even with the captured weapons, he had no chance of outgunning or outrunning six men. These Gila Rangers did not panic as the others had. They fanned out, intending to cut off his escape to either flank. That left only straight downhill open, unless he found a place to make his stand.

Slocum had been in enough fights to know the man below had twice the fight on his hands as one on higher ground shooting down. He stumbled and fell. He rolled away from two slugs seeking his back. Slocum painfully

pulled himself behind a lightning-struck stump and decided he had to make his stand there.

His knee hurting from the fall, he braced a rifle on the
stump and fired until it came up empty. The next rifle
jammed on the first shot. Slocum cast it aside and knew
death was coming after him—fast. He hefted the third rifle
and fired, winging one of his attackers.

Before he could get off another shot, it sounded as if
he had been dropped into the middle of a full-scale battle.
From either flank ripped bullets. He hunkered down, wondering if Walker's men had gotten confused, one group
firing on the other attacking him. Slocum wasn't going to
tell them about it. He looked for a way out, but saw two
men coming up the hill behind him.

He was caught, nowhere to run.

Slocum hefted his rifle, sighting in on one man below
him. He had a small advantage given him by elevation
and had to use it. Before he squeezed off the killing shot,
a familiar voice spoke behind him.

"That's not such a good idea, Slocum. Drop the rifle if
you want to keep on living. And I assure you, if you kill
my good buddy Finn, you're dead no matter what else
happens."

Slocum took in myriad details. The stench of gunpowder hung in the air, mixed with the sharp, coppery tang
of spilled blood. The echoes of the gunfight died down.
Here and there came weak moans. The fight uphill from
him was over, decided by the man speaking to him.

"You got me, Yarrow," he said, laying the rifle down.
If Yarrow had wanted him dead, he would have shot, not
spoken.

"So I do. But just what it is I have gotten, as you say,
is something of a mystery."

"Tell Walker I'll cut his heart out if I find him," Slocum
said, turning to face Yarrow. The man looked as crisp and
well-groomed as if he had just walked out of a barbershop

after a bath and shave. The way he held his two six-guns in rock-steady hands confirmed what Slocum had already guessed.

Yarrow was accomplished with those six-shooters. The calluses were those of a gunman, not a snake-oil salesman or tinkerer or even a gambler.

"Why'd you shoot your own men? Or are you having a falling out with Walker?" asked Slocum.

"You have some odd notions, Slocum," Yarrow said. The man thrust his six-shooters back into a wide leather belt, cross-draw style. Slocum had seen men using this way of carrying their guns who were faster than a striking snake. Yarrow moved so that he gave the impression of looking down on such men as being woefully sluggish.

"You're not with the Gila Rangers, are you?" Yarrow asked.

Slocum spat.

"I take that as a definitive answer. Not often I'm wrong. I had you pegged as a robber, and a good one. Thought you were riding with Walker."

As Yarrow spoke, a puff of wind carried back the tails of his coat, revealing a shining federal marshal's badge on his vest.

"I'm a marshal," he said, looking down to see what had startled Slocum. "Thought you had that figured out already."

"I thought you and Walker were in cahoots."

"Been trying to get the goods on him for some time." As Yarrow spoke, his men assembled. He had a dozen men, all sporting deputies' badges. Slocum recognized a few of them, two having ridden out to José's way station with Yarrow. "He's a slippery one. He seldom takes part in a robbery himself, preferring to send a lieutenant to do the dirty work. We can chop off the finger, but the brain still connives."

"So you are holding off, letting the Gila Rangers raid at will, trying to nab Walker?"

"Something like that, but I have bigger fish to fry."

"Sheriff Hardeen?" guessed Slocum.

"I do declare, you are a bright one. How did I ever mistake you for an outlaw?" Yarrow's cold gaze told Slocum the lawman had accurately sized him up. It was only unpredictable fate that Slocum was not riding with the Gila Rangers.

"Walker or one of his men gutshot my partner. Someone's going to pay for that. Walker's tried to kill me himself a time or two. He'll pay for that. And—"

"And you and Miss Reilly have formed, umm, an alliance to recover the gold taken from her bank. Or is that her uncle's bank?"

"It's her bank," Slocum said, seeing very little passed Yarrow by. He wasn't fooling the marshal one bit about his reasons for helping Grace.

"What were you two doing out here?"

"I had found the Gila Rangers' old camp a few miles yonder," Slocum said, pointing in the direction where Walker had camped before. "Grace had overheard one of Walker's men talking about Esqueleto Mesa. We were on our way there when we were ambushed."

"We just came from there," Yarrow said. "No hideout. Walker has been in these mountains long enough to know every cave and valley."

"But those men!" protested Slocum, pointing to the bodies on the ground and the ones Yarrow's deputies had captured. "That proves Walker is around somewhere."

Yarrow shook his head. "They were on their way back from a robbery up north. We recovered almost a thousand dollars they got from a train robbery holdup."

"So Walker doesn't know any of this happened? That his men got shot up?"

"No." Yarrow stared at Slocum, cold eyes boring into

him. Slocum returned the gaze. If Yarrow had seen a
wanted poster on him, he would be penned up with Walker's men, not debating what the next move ought to be
with the federal marshal himself.

"What's Walker planning?" Slocum asked.

"You *are* a quick study, Slocum," said Yarrow, admiration coming into his voice. "If I tell you, what will you
do?"

"I want to see Walker dead. If not that, in jail."

"Good enough," said Yarrow. He motioned for Slocum
to accompany him as they hiked back up the hill to the
game trail Slocum and Grace had followed when they had
been ambushed. At the top, the marshal looked around,
as if expecting to see someone spying on them.

He finally straightened his shoulders and began his
story. "Fort Carleton is doubling the size of its contingent.
The army is getting ready to start a major war against the
Apache and needs the fort as a secure supply point."

"Hadn't heard," Slocum said, his mind racing. "More
soldiers means more pay, which means payroll being
shipped in."

"Walker is going to rob the courier bringing in the payroll—in gold. I want to nab him before that happens."

"How big is the payroll?" asked Slocum, his old in-
stincts coming to the fore.

"Very. I don't know the precise size, but it'll be over
five thousand in gold coins. It's intended to last for a
while, paying the wages for five hundred cavalrymen, in
addition to monetary reserves for buying supplies to keep
them in the field, for a year. The army intends to make
this a major campaign, and doesn't want anything to slow
it until the last of the Apaches are on the San Carlos
reservation."

Slocum said nothing about the gold Walker had already
stolen from Grace's bank. If Yarrow didn't know about

it—or didn't care—that gave Slocum and Tolliver an opportunity to ride off with it.

"What do you want from me?" Slocum asked.

"I'm not looking to deputize you," Yarrow said, laughing. "You don't look like the badge-wearing kind to me. I want your eyes and ears, Slocum. I've watched how you talk to men and how you listen to what they are saying. Most folks are intent only on hearing their own voices."

"Information? That's all you want from me?"

"What else can you offer?"

"I'm not sure, but maybe there is one thing. Do you intend to trail the wagon with the payroll?"

Yarrow shrugged. "Haven't decided."

"Walker would spot your men if you trailed the wagon loaded with the gold. Too big a detachment of soldiers, and he won't attack. Too small and he'll get curious. Either way, you lose him."

"You obviously have a plan in mind. What is it?"

"Let's get back to Neutral," Slocum said. "I need to talk with Grace Reilly. It might be we can bait a trap for Walker. When he springs it, you and your deputies can be waiting."

"I'm interested," Yarrow said. He waved and got a couple men out to find Slocum's horse. As they rode back to Neutral, Slocum thought hard on the plan. It seemed good to him. Really good.

"A federal marshal?" Grace's eyebrows shot up. She pushed a strand of her coppery hair from her eyes and stared wide-eyed at Yarrow. "I had no idea."

"You weren't supposed to, Miss Reilly. If everyone in Neutral knew I was the law, Walker would have either moved on or shot me in the back."

"What can I do?" she asked.

"Slocum's got a cockeyed idea about luring Walker into robbing your bank."

"Again," she said bitterly. She caught Slocum's eye. He shook his head slightly, warning her not to go into too much detail about the gold theft.

"The bank's in mighty sorry condition after Grace's uncle blew it up," Slocum said. "We need to get it rebuilt to make this credible. Walker would never believe the army would put a gold shipment into a burned-down adobe hut unless it was going to be secure."

"The vault is intact," Grace said. "I checked on that."

"Then all you need is to get the bank itself in decent condition," Yarrow said. "Slocum's plan calls for the courier's wagon to break down. While it's being fixed, the soldiers guarding the gold shipment store it in your bank. Temporary, just overnight, but Walker's sure to know since he'll be watching the shipment."

Something niggled at Slocum's mind. Grace had said something he didn't understand, but he had other points to toss into the hopper about his scheme to catch Walker.

"A big company of soldiers is guarding the gold on its way through Neutral," he said. "Big enough to keep Walker at bay. Then, while the gold is 'safe' in the bank, most of the soldiers go riding off on some mission."

"I can arrange for word of an Apache attack to get to Neutral about the same time," said Yarrow. "It's plausible to think an officer, bored with guarding gold and intent on winning a medal or promotion, might split his force and go off to kill Apaches."

"Good, Marshal, that is very good," said Grace. "So the gold is locked up in the bank but guarded by only a few soldiers."

"Walker comes for the gold, and my men and I arrest him and the rest of the Gila Rangers. With luck, we can get Hardeen too."

"You have to be sure Walker will be with the robbers," Slocum said. "You told me he sent lieutenants so he would be lily-white."

"A robbery this big means the army sending a half-dozen companies to get their payroll back. Walker will want to steal the gold himself and hightail it straight south across the border." Yarrow nodded to himself as he played with the details. Everything clicked. Slocum could see how pleased the federal marshal was by the expression on his face.

But something wasn't quite right. Slocum had almost put his finger on it when Yarrow derailed the train of thought.

"You might need to carry the information to him, Slocum. Could you do that?"

"He wouldn't trust me," Slocum said. "There's bad blood between us."

"Don't tell him. Let him overhear it. You and your partner—Tolliver—might be sitting in the Dead Lizard talking about what you heard from Miss Reilly. One of the Gila Rangers gets it back to him and—*voila!* We have him sticking his head in the noose."

"John can do that," Grace said quickly.

"We need to get your uncle's approval before we go ahead with this, contacting the army about what we intend," said Slocum. "Legally, Matthew Reilly still runs the bank. Him making a big fuss would put the plan in jeopardy." Slocum looked at Yarrow, and saw a flare of skepticism on the marshal's face at the mention of Grace's uncle. Slocum figured Yarrow knew about Reilly and Walker's argument before the bank blew up.

"Uncle Matthew will agree. Why shouldn't he?"

"He and Walker have had a run-in," Slocum agreed. "I don't know the details, but I overheard them arguing. There's no love lost between the two of them. That's probably why Reilly booby-trapped the bank, knowing Walker would try to rob him."

"And how he would go about it," mused Yarrow. "Reilly had a good idea precisely how Walker would strike at him. I got a hint of that background for the men too. It doesn't sound like they are in cahoots, though. You saw them arguing, Slocum. Perhaps Walker robbed a bank Reilly ran over in California. I doubt they were partners. If anything, Reilly would enjoy seeing Walker behind bars."

"I'm sure that is true," Grace said. "Uncle Matthew is a very honest man. What his dealings with Walker might have been, I don't know, but we can work it out. I am sure. Oh, this is going to be good! Walker and the terrible vigilantes of his all arrested. And Sheriff Hardeen! After they are imprisoned, the bank will do *so* well!"

Slocum did not share Grace's enthusiasm because he was missing some small detail. His pa had always told him, "Son, the devil is in the details."

The devil stalked among the details—the one eluding Slocum.

15

Slocum scratched his head as he watched the workmen sweating in the hot sun. Eight men struggled to lift a twelve-foot-long viga into place while two more workmen crouched on the bank roof, struggling to guide the heavy beam into position. When it sank into place with a dull thud, the roof was finished, save for the thatching. That could be done by less-skilled carpenters.

"How are the iron bars?" Slocum asked the foreman of the project. The man mopped sweat and glanced up. He recognized Slocum as someone who usually had Grace Reilly with him, and thus ought to be worth spending a few minutes explaining things to.

"Cain't rightly say it'll hold if anyone's determined. The pair of rods in the back-room ceiling look like somebody whumped on 'em with an ax. But they are solid. Look like iron brought in from the ironworks up in Pueblo, Colorado." He turned back to work, striving to get burned wood out of the lobby. The entire renovation would be finished in another day, preparing the bank for business.

And the cavalry gold shipment.

And the trap Marshal Yarrow was going to spring on the Gila Rangers.

Slocum stepped over piles of debris and went into the back room, where the sooty vault stood like a valiant sentry. He swung the doors back and forth a few times. The screeching sound begged for oil, but the hinges were solid and the locking bars moved easily inside the heavy doors. Once locked, the safe would again provide a secure repository for gold or the life savings of the townspeople.

He frowned as he moved the double doors. Sturdy. Invulnerable. It would take a case of dynamite to blast open the vault. Perfect for the marshal's trap.

Perfect. So what was wrong?

"You, Slocum, what are you doing here?" came Matthew Reilly's gruff question. "I don't want to see you hanging around my bank. Clear out. Now!"

"Whatever you say, Mr. Reilly," Slocum said, not wanting to argue with Grace's uncle. The man was as arrogant and obnoxious as his brother. Slocum started to leave, then spun around when Reilly grabbed his shoulder.

"You're a bank robber, aren't you?" Reilly said.

"What's your beef with Walker?" Slocum shot back. The banker's eyes widened, then went squinty.

"There's nothing between us. He runs the vigilantes responsible for keeping the peace in this town. I want to get along with him. That's all."

"See you around," Slocum said, jerking free of the banker's meaty hand. Reilly sputtered, then shouted unintelligibly as Slocum stepped into the dusty street running the length of Neutral. Pulling down the brim of his floppy hat, Slocum watched three men he knew were Gila Rangers riding to a hitching post in front of a saloon. The trio dismounted and went inside, bold as brass.

Then Slocum caught himself. In his mind he had them caught and convicted by Marshal Yarrow. Until Walker showed up and helped rob the cavalry gold shipment, the vigilantes would have the run of the town, acting like cocks of the walk.

Slocum went to Dr. Martin's surgery and poked his head inside, expecting to find Clay Tolliver. The bed was neatly made and only the doctor was inside. Martin turned bloodshot eyes on Slocum.

"You're lettin' in the heat. Go or stay, I don't much c-care."

"Where's my partner?"

"Tolliver? Ain't—haven't seen him since yesterday. Can't rightly say where he went."

"He pay up?" Slocum doubted Dr. Martin would be so easy about losing his live-in patient if Tolliver had not paid. Slocum's partner had plenty of money, the green-backs stolen back from the Gila Rangers.

"Yep. Missy Grace paid fer the varmint a long time back." The doctor hiccuped loudly, reached into a bottom desk drawer, and pulled out a full bottle of rye. This told Slocum how the physician had been spending the money.

"Know where I can find him?" Slocum asked.

"Nope."

Slocum saw the doctor was deep in his cups and wasn't likely to give any more information. He left the surgery, considered checking the saloons, and decided that was not too good an idea. The Gila Rangers were pouring into town now, to size up the newly repaired bank and to position themselves for the gold robbery. Yarrow had started the rumors flying about how big the gold shipment was likely to be. Even otherwise honest men opined how they would spend the gold, if it happened to come their way.

He had to admit, if he had not known it was a trap, Slocum would have been drawn to it like flies to a fresh cow flop. There would be a risk; every outlaw knew that up front. That there would be a company or more of armed, wary soldiers guarding the gold was a certainty. From there, Yarrow's plan had to rely on what seemed logical happenstance to Walker.

Slocum sat in the shade, watched the entry of the Gila

Rangers into Neutral, and thought on gold. Lots of gold. The shipment was not bogus and was intended to supply Fort Carleton for a year or more. Slocum wondered if it might be possible to steal the cavalry's gold, blame it on the Gila Rangers, and escape into Mexico without getting Yarrow down on his neck.

Yarrow had everything too well sewn up for that. Slocum gave up plotting and started thinking on other things, the heat diffusing his thoughts and letting his mind run wild. Again, he returned to something wrong about the bank, about the safe, about how Walker had stolen the mining consortium's new hoard of gold and almost ruined Grace's reputation.

"Buy you a drink, Slocum?"

"You're mighty hospitable," Slocum said to the federal marshal. "You think that's smart? I counted fifteen Gila Rangers in town already."

"I reckon you're right. Keep yourself out of trouble." Yarrow glanced down the street to where Sheriff Hardeen dragged along a drunken miner, heading for the county lockup.

"How are you drawing him into the web?" Slocum asked.

"He's the one I'm going to tell that the captain in charge is sneaking out to go save settlers from the Apache. Only the sheriff will know three men are left to guard the bank and the gold."

"When's the shipment due?"

"Tomorrow. By around noon or soon after that, the wagon'll break down and the troopers will have it into town by sundown."

Matthew Reilly blustered and harrumphed his way along the street, pushing mere citizens out of his way. Slocum saw the banker as a weak link in the chain, but Yarrow held to his belief that Reilly would not cave in to Walker.

The plan depended on too many details to suit Slocum,

but there might be a spot where he could make off with at least some of the gold. No matter how he looked at it, a pile of gold coins was far superior to a mail sack stuffed with greenbacks.

Especially in Mexico.

Yarrow sauntered off to plant his seeds in the nearest saloon. Slocum turned toward the steep hill where Grace's house perched on the crest. Hiking in the hot sun took the stuffing out of him. By the time he reached the front porch, he wanted nothing more than a bucket of cool water.

"Grace!" he called. Slocum knocked on the front door. "You home?"

He'd started to knock again when he heard a horse out back. Slocum went around the house in time to see Grace riding down a winding trail leading toward the Gila Road. He took a few quick steps, waved, and shouted. She was too far off to hear.

Too far down the trail and riding hard. Where did Grace ride in such a powerful hurry?

Slocum decided he wanted to know. He couldn't find his partner in town, and now Grace Reilly had lit out like someone had set fire to her toes. He made his way back down the steep hill, crossed the street, and walked briskly to the stables. Yarrow ought to know he was leaving town, but Slocum did not want to pass along the information to the marshal. To have done so might draw unwanted attention. Right now it was better the Gila Rangers think everything was running according to Walker's plan.

Anything unusual might spook Walker into running. The outlaw had the gold stolen from the bank the night Reilly blew it up, but that was only a taste of what he might steal from the U.S. Army.

Slocum saddled his protesting horse, then rode past the Butterfield Stage office. The station agent waved to him as he rode past. Slocum returned the greeting, then swung west along the Gila Road, estimating where the backtrail from Grace's house might join the road.

It took him a half hour longer than anticipated before he found the woman's tracks. Slocum stood in the stirrups and tried to see a dust cloud ahead along the road to show where Grace rode. Nothing. Slocum wondered if the extra half hour it had taken him to follow and reach this point had given her the chance to get away.

Away to where? Slocum did not like Grace holding out on him, and she obviously had important business about which he knew nothing. Might be something innocent, he knew. She had said there was a spot in the nearby foothills where she enjoyed going. But the timing was bad for such picnics.

The trap was being set. Anything might warn off Walker, and that included Grace riding along the Gila Road where the wagon load of gold would rattle along in about twenty-four hours.

As he walked his horse along the road, Slocum thought on how much money might be in that shipment. Enough to live like a king in Mexico. He could buy a lifetime of tequila and *pulque* and still have plenty left over for beans and tortillas.

He and Grace and Tolliver could all live like European royalty on that wagon filled with gold.

"Where are you going, Grace?" he whispered. "And what happened to you, Tolliver?" His horse neighed, tossed its head, and peered back at him. He dismounted, walked the horse a spell, but kept thinking. It felt as if he had jumped onto a log rolling free in the middle of a river. He could run and the log would turn under him, but he wouldn't get anywhere. But Slocum saw no way of slowing down the spin and stopping long enough to catch his breath and get a good look around him.

"Not doing so bad," he told himself. "That sack of scrip will be enough to keep us going for a long time." Whether

Grace would come along when she had a bank to run, even one destined to fail soon, was something Slocum did not want to dwell on.

He and Tolliver had been partners long enough to know that the money would do them both a world of good, Grace Reilly along for the ride or not.

It was past noon when Slocum got off the dusty trail and led his horse to the top of a ridge paralleling the Gila Road. He peered west along a five-mile stretch of road. Empty as a rich man's promise of charity. No one rode out on the desert that Slocum could see. He might have been the only man left alive on Earth.

Slocum settled down in the shade of a tall boulder, letting his horse rest and giving himself a break. After twenty minutes, Slocum headed back to Neutral, knowing his chances of finding Grace had vanished when he had lost sight of her on the trail behind her house. When he reached the place where it branched off the Gila Road and curved its way to the rear of the woman's house, Slocum rode uphill.

His horse complained all the way until they reached Grace's house in late afternoon. She was still gone. Slocum fed and watered his horse in the woman's barn, caught a short nap, and still she was not back. Darkness slipped down on Neutral, forcing the saloon owners to light the gas lamps in front of their drinking establishments. Slocum watched one torch after another flare into life.

He led his horse out of the barn and down the road in front of Grace's house until he was just out of sight. He tethered the horse on a mesquite, then hiked back to the woman's house and sat on the front porch. The sounds of merriment from town came drifting up on a soft evening breeze. Smells of stale beer and spilled whiskey lured Slocum to town, but he waited.

He leaned back and closed his eyes. He drifted off to

sleep, only to come awake when he heard the clop-clop of hooves behind the house. Slocum checked his watch and saw it was almost midnight. Grace had been gone most of the day.

Where?

Asking her would only give her the chance to lie to him. Deep down Slocum knew Grace would not tell the truth, and the lie would be obvious. Lights came on inside the house. He sat on the porch, wondering what he should do.

As the woman went upstairs and the light in her bedroom came on, Slocum left the porch, got on the winding road leading back into Neutral, and caught up the reins for his horse. He led the horse back to the livery stable he and the horse called home, tended the animal, then spread out his blanket and tried to get to sleep.

He had too many questions and not enough answers to go to sleep easily.

16

"Isn't this a mite risky?" asked Slocum. Marshal Yarrow rode a few feet ahead of him, eager to get on with the capture of the vigilantes. Behind them fanned out a small army of federal deputies. Slocum turned from Yarrow to look down the Gila Road where a heavily laden wagon rattled along. Flanking it rode orderly twin columns of a full company of cavalry, a flapping gold and blue pennon at the front.

Old habits died hard in Slocum. A Federal captain commanded the company. Slocum longed for his rifle and a good shot. He shook off the notion he could keep on killing Yankee officers. The war was over, and well done, he knew. But rather than deciding another in a meaningless series of skirmishes, this shot might win him the contents of the wagon. Gold beyond his dreams of avarice.

"My boys say that Walker is biding his time, drinking it up in the Sundog Saloon," said Yarrow.

"Might have a few scouts out to watch the gold's progress," Slocum said. He scanned the horizon and saw nothing but relentless heat shimmer on the desert and an occasional dust devil swirling mindlessly. "If one of the Gila Rangers spots us, the trap isn't going to work."

"You worry too much, Slocum. There's nothing that will drive off Walker once he gets the scent of this much gold. It's going to pull him straight into a trap—and Yuma Penitentiary."

Slocum said nothing. Walker might be greedy, but he was no fool. Going up against a handful of soldiers was one thing; knowing a small army of federal deputies waited for him was something else. So far, Yarrow had no hard evidence against Walker that would stand up in court. It was too much to hope Yarrow wanted to catch Walker and then string him up on the nearest cottonwood like the outlaw had done to those two drifters.

Slocum could almost forgive the way Walker had killed Utah Jaeger and his two partners. There was no honor among thieves. But the drifters had done nothing wrong, other than crossing the Gila Rangers' trail at the worst time possible. In a way, Slocum felt responsible for their deaths since Walker might not have killed them if he had not been showing off.

"Let's you and me ride on down and talk to the captain," Yarrow said. "It's about time for the wagon to break down."

"It's a couple miles to town. That's a long ways to go with a crippled wagon that is so heavily loaded."

"Exactly," Yarrow said. "If Walker got scent of a trap, he'd expect it to happen in town. This way, he won't think we'd work so hard to catch him. Breaking down out here looks real."

"Looks mighty hot too," Slocum said. He swiped at sweat, then took a long pull from his canteen.

Yarrow gave orders to his deputies. One trotted back in the direction of Neutral, probably to report the supposed Apache depredations to Sheriff Hardeen and prime that pump. By the time the captain and his soldiers reached town, the sheriff would be sure the Indians were on the way to burn Neutral to the ground. The captain's quest for glory in battle rather than wet-nursing a load of gold would be reasonable and maybe even demanded by an outraged, fearful Neutral populace.

By the time Hardeen told Walker what was going on, the Gila Rangers' leader would think he'd died and gone to heaven.

Slocum and Yarrow waved to the lead scout in the column, who passed word back to his commander. The captain trotted out on a fine-looking black stallion that tossed its head and remained strong and fit even after a long trip through the hot desert. Slocum envied the captain his horse.

There his admiration stopped. The arrogant officer looked down his nose at Slocum, and barely acknowledged Yarrow's greeting.

"This is the most harebrained scheme I have ever been privy to," the captain said without even saying howdy.

"Haven't been in the army long, Captain?" asked Slocum, not trying to keep the sarcasm from his voice. The officer glared at Slocum, pure hatred in his eyes. From the set of his body, the way he moved, everything about his meticulously tailored uniform, this was not a man who took orders easily from anyone not above him in the chain of command. To listen to a civilian would be worse than being staked out in the hot sun by Apaches.

"I have been ordered to do as you have requested, Marshal," the captain said stiffly.

"Then you get the nut loosened on the rear wheel. Send a man into town to find a wheelwright. Tell your courier it will be all right to go into a saloon and partake of a drink or two, letting it slip about the shipment and the predicament you find yourself in."

"We might as well *give* these road agents the gold."

"Be glad to take it off your hands, Captain," Slocum said. He could not stop himself from needling the man. "That'll give you the chance to fight Injuns."

"That is honorable work, even if I will be in command of Negroes once I reach the fort." The captain's stiffness increased until Slocum thought someone had shoved a ramrod up his butt.

"You're going to find the buffalo soldiers are better than any other unit you've commanded," Yarrow said, as irritated as Slocum.

"I will *make* them into the finest unit in the territory," the captain said.

Slocum was hot and uncomfortable and wanted to warn Yarrow against arguing at length with the officer. The marshal might not think Walker was smart enough to have scouts watching for the gold shipment, but Slocum did not want to take chances. Too much rode on this until they got the gold into the bank vault.

He frowned, again something he had missed fluttering at the edges of his mind, teasing him like a light feather touch, just beyond his reach and understanding.

"We can fake the loose nut, sir," said the captain.

"Get the wheel loosened," Yarrow said. "I want that wheel about ready to fall off when you get into Neutral."

"Neutral," sneered the captain. "What kind of name is that?"

"It's where you'll win your promotion to major," Yarrow said, finding the man's soft underbelly of conceit and digging in hard there. "Do this and you will have rid the territory of one of the most vicious gangs of outlaws since the Arizona Cowboys terrorized Tombstone."

"Very well. Sergeant! As ordered, right rear wheel nut! Loosen!"

"See you in town, Captain," said Yarrow. He and Slocum circled wide through the desert and approached Neutral from the south, keeping their eyes peeled for any sign of the Gila Rangers. The vigilantes had gone to ground, all gathered in Neutral to await the gold shipment.

"They figure they will get it out of the bank," Yarrow

said. "Even if they have to take on the entire company of soldiers, Walker will send them all into the fight."

"That road we crossed," Slocum said. "The one that was hardly a double-rut. Does it lead straight to Mexico?"

"Straight as an arrow. No sign of the Gila Rangers along it that I saw." Yarrow cocked his head to one side and looked at Slocum. "You see any of them?"

"Nope," said Slocum. That was the road he intended taking when he finished with Walker. If the opportunity arose, he would be riding along the road loaded down with gold in his saddlebags too. But right now, with so many soldiers and deputy marshals in and around Neutral, he saw no way of stealing any of the gold.

They rode to the edge of town, arriving at the same time the captain and his company did.

"Where's the wagon?" asked Slocum. "You don't think that jackass rode on ahead and left the wagon out on the road unguarded?"

Yarrow muttered under his breath, then galloped off cursing a blue streak. Slocum rode hard and fast after him to get to the wagon with its wobbling back wheel.

The virtually unguarded wagon.

"Stupid son of a bitch might as well have left them naked," Yarrow said angrily. "And there's big trouble brewing." He pointed to a dry wash a quarter mile down the road where two riders waited anxiously.

Slocum shielded his eyes, but could not make out who the riders were. But he could tell they wore masks.

"There are only two. Walker wouldn't risk his own neck like this," Slocum said.

"Might be a couple of his men who decided to go out on their own. They might have heard how Walker intended robbing the bank and decided to get their share before it even reached town."

"With the cavalry protection riding ahead, they might be able to help themselves."

"Over my dead body," Yarrow said, drawing his Winchester from its saddle sheath. Slocum duplicated the effort, and rode hard until he reached a spot ahead of the wagon where they could lay down fire into the wash. They turned and aimed.

The two robbers fired wildly at them. Yarrow and Slocum shot back with far more accuracy, for all the good that did. The two road agents fired wildly, spooking their own mounts and making it well nigh impossible for an accurate shot on either side.

"Surrender!" shouted Yarrow. "I'm a federal marshal, and you're under arrest for attempted robbery of a federal shipment!"

This produced exactly the result Slocum had thought it would. The two turned their horses up the sandy wash and rode hellbent for leather. He braced his rifle on his left forearm and sighted. He had one good shot at the trailing robber. His finger came back slowly, then relaxed. He could not fire.

"They're getting away," Slocum called to Yarrow. The marshal fought his bucking horse, trying to get his six-shooter around to wing or kill one of the would-be robbers. He gave up and got his horse under control. "It's not a good idea to chase them."

"Why not?" demanded Yarrow. Then the marshal settled down and glared. "You're right, Slocum. I hate to let them go, though."

"It might be a diversion, a way of getting us to show our hand before we're ready."

"Or to lure us into a trap so the rest of the Gila Rangers can pounce on the wagons. Damn that captain! Why'd he take off for town like that, leaving the gold behind?"

"Glory," Slocum said. "He's got victory in his eyes and guarding a shipment is garrison work to him, beneath his dignity."

"He might even buy into the Apache story," Yarrow

said in disgust. He glared in the direction taken by the two inept robbers, then circled his horse around and rejoined the wagon with its precariously wobbling wheel.

Slocum looked after the fleeing highwaymen with some curiosity. No robber worth his salt could have thought for a second he would succeed with a robbery that bumbling and inept. The only thought he had was how hot the sun was and perhaps it had cooked a pair of brains into believing it possible to grab the gold.

But how had they found out about the gold?

Slocum snorted and shook his head. He had been right not to shoot.

"We'd better make ourselves scarce, Slocum," said the marshal. "Wouldn't do for Walker to spot us with the gold shipment."

"Your men ready for the fight? It'll be a corker. Walker will hang on like a bulldog."

"They're experienced lawmen. I recruited them from all over the territory."

Slocum and Yarrow rode into town from the south while the wagon with its minimal guard barely made it in from the west along the Gila Road. Slocum fed and watered his horse and brushed it down. Somehow, he was not surprised to see Tolliver's horse missing from the next stall. Slocum had started to dig around in the piles of horse manure for the sack with the loot they had taken from Walker when Yarrow entered.

"Slocum!" the marshal called. "We got big problems. Real big ones."

"What's that?"

"There's been an Apache attack east of town."

"That's the story you planted with Hardeen. That's the reason the captain and most of his troopers won't be standing guard over the gold in the bank." Slocum stared at the marshal and saw the strained expression on his face.

"There *was* an attack. The captain rode into an ambush not a mile outside town."

"The Gila Rangers?" asked Slocum. He knew how easy it would be for something to go wrong with this plan. Walker finding out and ambushing the soldiers was the easiest explanation.

"Real Apaches, real deaths. The captain's dead, along with half his men. I don't have any choice. If I don't send my deputies out, the Indians might attack Neutral. Word is they are already preying on miners living along the far fringes of town."

"Walker," Slocum said. "He's making this up to draw away your men. He found out somehow and—"

"Here," Yarrow said, tossing a broken arrow to Slocum. Slocum examined it and chewed on his lower lip. He had seen arrows like this before. War arrows. Apache. From the look of this one, it was recently made.

"If you pull out your deputies, that lets Walker take the gold," Slocum said.

"We might not be any worse off than just keeping the gold in the bank overnight," Yarrow said. "There are four troopers who'll stand guard. I'll stay too. Can I count on you?"

"It'll be us against a couple dozen Gila Rangers," Slocum pointed out.

"Don't think so. A lot of them have formed a real vigilante committee to protect Neutral. Walker might not lead them, but most of his men are going to fight Indians."

It didn't sound right to Slocum. He wondered if this was some plot on Yarrow's part to steal the gold for himself. How much did a federal marshal earn in a month for risking his life? Fifty dollars? Probably not even that much.

The scheme had fallen apart fast. The captain had ridden off to glory—and his own death. Taking so many of his troopers with him had put the gold shipment at risk.

But the Apaches might have swept through town already if the captain had not ridden out when he had.

"They're barricading the streets and trying to put up a defense."

"You're sure about the Apaches?" asked Slocum.

"Dead sure. That was taken out of the back of my chief deputy—and a damned good friend, to boot."

"Sorry," said Slocum. His mind churned, but there were too many questions and niggling details he could not fit together to make it possible for him to take the gold for himself.

Gunshots from the far end of town told Slocum something was up.

"Shadows, they're shooting at shadows," the marshal said. "The Apache don't like to attack at night."

"Snakes," Slocum said. He knew the Apaches had a mortal fear of snakes, but they would attack if the stakes were high enough. Looting an entire town was a change in their tactics, but with a new war chief out to prove himself, anything was possible.

Slocum pulled his rifle from his gear and stuffed a box of ammo into his shirt pocket until the lump over his heart felt cold and hard.

"It'll be sunup in a few hours," the marshal said. "We can hold out that long."

"So? What happens then?"

"I'll know if my deputies chased off the Indians or if we're going to make a stand, building by building."

Slocum and Yarrow hurried toward the bank to add their guns to those of the four soldiers. It amazed Slocum how fast the plan had changed from arresting Walker and Hardeen to simply staying alive. Protect the gold if they could, but stay alive to fight another day.

"You men see anything unusual?" Yarrow asked of the corporal in charge.

"Nothing, sir," the corporal answered. "The bank's

safe. Let me take the squad out to the fighting."

"The gold," Yarrow chided, "guard the gold. You'll get a bellyful of killing before daybreak."

The corporal grumbled but obeyed. That much went smoothly. And that turned out to be about all.

Walker and six Gila Rangers struck a half hour later, riding up with guns blazing. Slocum and Yarrow were at the rear of the bank and missed the initial attack. By the time they ran around to add their firepower to that of the soldiers, the corporal and another soldier lay dead on the ground. The other two troopers bled from minor wounds.

"Where'd they go?" demanded Yarrow.

"That way, sir," grated out a private. "They went round back of that there saloon."

"Wait!" Slocum's warning did not stop Yarrow from running after Walker and his outlaws. Slocum looked around, wondering if the marshal was being decoyed. When he spotted the two robbers from along the road, he lit out after them.

The two saw him and bolted again. And again Slocum did not fire on them. He knew them, or thought he did. He skidded to a halt and returned to the bank, not sure what to do. He and two wounded soldiers were all that stood between law and a gold theft.

"Slocum, what are you doing here?" demanded Matthew Reilly, huffing and puffing up. The banker clutched a six-shooter, its barrel smoking. "I was down the street fighting off the Apaches."

"They're attacking?" Slocum turned to look. He heard Marshal Yarrow cry out a warning, and then Slocum fell facedown in the dusty street, struck on the head from behind.

A sharp crack sounded. A shot from a six-gun. Reilly's pistol? Half-dazed, Slocum rolled onto his side and saw Reilly fire on the federal marshal. Yarrow had tried to warn him about the banker. Slocum tried to raise his six-gun and shoot Reilly, but his nerveless hand would not obey.

He watched the banker gun down the marshal, then turn and kill the two stunned soldiers. Reilly grinned from ear to ear, then went around the bank, returning quickly with a pair of horses.

He was going to rob his own bank!

Slocum struggled to sit up, but his head spun in wild, crazy orbits that forced him to lie down. He would recover his wits, then catch Reilly when he came from the bank. With Yarrow gone and the cavalry troopers dead, there was nothing to keep Slocum from robbing the bank. Let Reilly do the work, then—

Slocum played dead when three rifles fired simultaneously. The slugs ripped through Reilly as the banker struggled to heave the gold into the packs.

"You fools," came Walker's snarl. "You shoulda let him load the gold for us, then kill him. Get on over there. Take the gold. We got to get out of here 'fore the Apaches kill the lot of them fools fightin' 'em at the other end of town."

"Right, Boss."

Slocum watched through half-hooded eyes as three Gila Rangers lugged the gold from the bank and stuffed it into the packs Reilly had thought to use.

"All loaded, Boss!"

"Ride!" ordered Walker.

Slocum sat up fast, his six-shooter firing at the retreating Gila Rangers. He winged one of Walker's men, knocking him from the saddle. But he missed the other two vigilantes—and Walker. He missed the leader of the Gila Rangers by a country mile. Then it was too late. Walker, his men, and the gold-laden packhorse were swallowed up by the night.

Sitting in the dust, Slocum looked around him and seethed. Yarrow was down. Reilly was dead. Four troopers had been murdered. One of Walker's men had been wounded.

And Walker had ridden off with the army's gold.

Slocum's gold. He had earned it. He had fought for it, and by rights it ought to be his!

Furious at the turn of events, Slocum got to his feet, jumbled, jagged thoughts turning into a new plan. This time he wasn't going to be the one in the dust.

He would be the one with the gold and Walker would be buzzard bait under the burning Arizona sun.

17

Slocum stood over the outlaw he had winged. He put his boots on either side of the man's head, then turned his heels inward so the Spanish-rowled spurs cut into the man's cheeks. The Gila Ranger stirred and moaned. His eyes came open slowly. Then a look of sheer terror masked his face.

He looked straight up into the bore of Slocum's pistol. It was only a .36-caliber, but it had to look big enough to stuff his head into.

"Where's Walker taking the gold?" Slocum asked.

"I . . . I don't know."

"You're lying. In five seconds you are going to be lying and very, very dead." Slocum cocked the pistol and pointed it directly at the man's eyes. Not many men were brave enough to accept death. And Slocum offered nothing but a slug to the brain.

"Wait! I . . . I really don't know, but I think I know. There's a mesa out there."

"Esqueleto Mesa," Slocum said. "So?"

"Walker likes it. You can look down on the three trails leading up to it. He left our other camp in a hurry to go up there."

Slocum considered how likely it was the man was lying. He was pale and trembled. That could come from the bullet he had taken in the back. But there was no eye-darting or trying to look honest while lying. The outlaw had given Slocum all he was likely to get.

"Don't go anywhere," Slocum said. "The federal marshal will want to talk to you." This might not happen at all, depending on how badly injured Yarrow was. He had been ambushed, and Slocum had no desire to see if he was still alive.

The gold beckoned to him. *His* gold called to his avarice like a Siren.

Slocum stepped back, lowered the hammer on his Colt Navy, then spun and walked off. He got his horse and rode in the direction of Esqueleto Mesa, thinking on how likely Walker was to go somewhere the law already knew was a hideout.

It was something the outlaw would do, Slocum decided. Walker had not thought things would go so wrong, not that he cared who died. All the owlhoot wanted was the gold.

And again, something about the gold bothered Slocum. Reilly had known the combination and had opened the safe, so Walker did not have to blow it open. Reilly had died for his attempted theft. Slocum snorted at the idea that Grace's uncle was such an outright thief. It made sense that Matthew Reilly had once been in cahoots with Walker, maybe in California, possibly somewhere else. Slocum saw no difference between a man who held up another using a six-gun and a banker who stole by clever, duplicitous use of the law.

The only difference, perhaps, being that the one using the gun was somehow more honorable about his actions. Everyone recognized the road agent as being on the wrong side of the law. Only those robbed by the banker's slick schemes considered that double-dealing to be theft.

Slocum hunted for sign of Walker and the other riders, but saw nothing in the soft roadbed. He had to rely on his information being right that Walker was headed for Esqueleto Mesa. The turnoff from the Gila Road came on him suddenly—and there Slocum found his first spoor.

Fresh horse droppings showed someone had come that way within the past hour or two. Who else would ride this time of night? Dawn had yet to break, though light would soon flood across the desert again and turn Arizona into a furnace. Slocum intended to be far up into the cool mountains before that happened.

He pushed his horse to the limit, climbing steep hills and passing ponderosa and Apache pine. The wooded areas changed as he rode steadily, going to pinyon, and finally to aspen and scrub oak.

The trail led back and forth up the face of a cliff to Esqueleto Mesa. Slocum found more spoor. He also had the sense of being watched. He dismounted, pretending to study the trail but looking out the corners of his eyes for trouble.

He found it before it found him. A sniper had hidden down a steep slope leading to a spring runoff gully. He was worming his way up slowly, trying to get a better shot at Slocum.

Slocum stood, looked around, and saw no trace of the other Gila Rangers. This might be one of the road agents left behind to guard Walker's backtrail. If so, Walker was going to be alerted. Quick.

Spinning and going into a gunfighter's crouch, Slocum grabbed for his six-shooter. He drew and fired in one smooth movement. The move took the would-be sniper by surprise—and the slug caught him in the shoulder. The man let out a shriek of agony and flinched away.

This gave Slocum the time to step up to the lip of the road and point his six-gun directly at the man.

"Drop the rifle," Slocum ordered.

"You the law?"

"I'm your worst nightmare if you don't do what you're told," Slocum snapped.

The man reluctantly shoved the rifle away.

"I ain't done nothin'. You got no call to—"

"Is Walker up on the mesa?" Slocum asked.

"How'd you know?"

The man realized he was not going to get away without having his worthless hide ventilated further. He rolled and went for the six-shooter holstered at his right side. Slocum had plenty of time to drill him straight through the heart. By the time the man stopped rolling over and over, he was dead.

Slocum looked up to the mesa top. It was a hard ride, but he had to do it. Walker had left with three men, and Slocum had shot one out of the saddle. The dead owlhoot at the bottom of the gully meant only one man was still riding with Walker. But the leader of the Gila Rangers might have met up with others in his gang. Slocum dared not rely on Walker and one other being his only obstacles to overcome before he claimed the gold for his own.

Going down the slope a few feet, Slocum recovered the dead sniper's rifle. He needed all the firepower he could get. Mounting, Slocum began the ride up the steep trail, his horse protesting every step of the way. Slocum would have walked the horse up the trail normally, but now speed counted.

He had two main sources for his uneasiness. Walker might have more than one man still with him, making a shootout dangerous. The other problem Slocum might face was Walker hiding the gold where no one could ever find it. Esqueleto Mesa was big enough to afford hundreds of good hiding places.

Walker might also have buried the gold on the way to the top.

Slocum slowed when the trail broadened and leveled

out. He had reached the top of the mesa. He dropped to one side of the horse, using it as a shield against possible sniping. Losing his horse would be a real misfortune because the animal had responded every time he had asked for another few miles, a few feet, just another few minutes.

With the gold Walker had stolen, Slocum could buy a dozen horses just as good.

He walked out on the relatively level rocky surface of the mesa, noting the piles of boulders that might give Walker good hiding places for the gold or for an ambush. He ranged back and forth in a fan-shaped search pattern, looking for any hint where Walker, his sidekick, and the gold had gone. What he found brought a smile to his lips. Slocum reached down and picked up a small leather pouch.

Hefting it, he knew what was inside. Gold coins. Walker had somehow lost it. Or was he only baiting a trap? Slocum turned even more cautious as he followed the game trail on which the bag of gold had lain. The gold slapped gently against his leg as he walked, reminding him not to get too greedy.

Slocum levered a round into his captured rifle, then left his horse and cut directly left from the trail he followed. He went fifty yards, then turned to parallel the course he had been following. He smelled his opponent before he saw him. A tiny puff from a cigarette made his nose twitch and his mouth water.

It had been too long since he had been able to afford tobacco and all the fixings. Crouching, Slocum moved forward, but could not find whoever lay in wait for him. The trail had not been cut up, telling him only a few horses had passed by.

"It's me! Walker!" Slocum said in a low voice, hoping he'd imitated the Gila Ranger leader well enough to fool whoever was in ambush. The sounds of a man shifting his weight came from upwind, another clue he had flushed out his quarry. Sniffing again, Slocum caught a fresh whiff of the fragrant tobacco.

He flopped on his belly and waited.

"Where are you?" came the soft call. "I thought you tole me to wait 'n you'd come back at sundown. Where are you, Walker?"

The outlaw made no effort to step quietly. To Slocum's sensitive ears, it sounded more like a buffalo stampede than a single man approaching. Slocum's finger curled on the trigger, then relaxed. He did not want to kill this self-appointed vigilante, not without finding out where Walker had gone. From the brief exchange, Slocum figured Walker had abandoned this poor trusting fool and had high-tailed it with all the gold taken from the army.

"Walker?"

The man stopped a few paces from Slocum's hiding place. He scratched his head, then rested his rifle against a boulder to better tend his cigarette. The paper had split, spilling some of the shredded tobacco. The man snuffed out the smoke, then took out new rolling papers and started another cigarette.

Slocum circled and came up behind. "Mind if I bum one off you too?"

"Naw, I—" The man whirled about. Slocum swung as the man spun. The butt of the rifle caught the outlaw squarely on the chin. He went down as if he had been poleaxed.

"Damn," Slocum said. He had knocked the man out. Slocum picked up the fixings where the man had dropped them, then worked a spell to roll himself a smoke. He pulled out a lucifer and lit the cigarette, inhaling deeply. The smoke curled down into his lungs and gave him a sense everything was going well.

By the time the man shook his head, rubbed his jaw,

and then pushed up to one elbow, Slocum was ready for him.

"Where's Walker?" Slocum asked.

"Who're you?" The man rubbed his jaw, then his eyes. "You're Slocum, the one Walker's always goin' on about."

"Reckon I'm the one. I want to be Walker's worst nightmare, not yours. But I can be that too." Slocum aimed the rifle at the man to see his reaction. He might have been stupid when it came to being a sentry, but he showed more sand than the outlaw back at the bank. He blinked, and then resolve firmed to the point that Slocum thought he might have to torture the information from him.

"He's playing you for a sucker," Slocum said. "You got any of the gold?"

"I . . . no. What's that got to do with anythin'?" The question took the man by surprise.

"Here," Slocum said, tossing the leather bag of coins. "That's all you're ever going to see. Truth is, you won't even see the sunset if you don't tell me what I need to know."

"Walker said you were a mangy cayuse and would threaten me to scare me."

"Some advice. The federal marshal—his name's Yarrow—is on his way with a whale of a big posse made up of deputies. Nobody's going to get off this mesa that the marshal doesn't let off."

"Why are you telling me this?"

"I don't have a grudge against you. My beef's with Walker. He shot my partner, and he's done other things I need to even the score on."

"That banker?"

"That's part of it," Slocum said.

"Walker told me him and Reilly had rode together for a spell and that Reilly had turned him in to the law."

"Don't care," Slocum said, knowing that every minute they palavered, Walker rode another few yards farther beyond his reach. "Walker. Where'd he head?"

"You'll let me go?"

"You've got some gold. I'll tell you where Marshal Yarrow is coming from so you can avoid him and his posse. More 'n that, you're on your own."

The man considered his options, opened the leather bag and shook out a few of the gold coins, then shoved them back in.

"Due north. Walker's headed due north. Just him and the pack animal with the gold. He tole me he was gonna hide it where X marks the spot."

"What?"

The man shrugged. "That's what he tole me. Don't know more 'n that."

"Due north, eh?" Slocum motioned for the man to clear out. The outlaw got to his feet, then turned hesitantly, sure Slocum was going to shoot him in the back. When Slocum only sat, smoking and watching, the man lit out like his tail had been set on fire. Slocum finished the cigarette, then fetched his horse. He had a ways to go before he caught up with Walker.

"X marks the spot," he said, shaking his head in wonder. The outlaw had been brave enough, but dumber than dirt to expect Walker to ever cut him in on a haul like they had made in Neutral.

"Two loads of gold," Slocum reminded himself. "They emptied the vault before too. Now they got the army's gold. *Walker's* got the gold," he corrected himself.

As he rode along the trail, he saw more and more indications that Walker and another horse had passed by. One horse made deeper indentations, showing it carried several hundred pounds—of gold.

The trail curved near a huge boulder, then angled away to the north. Slocum watched the ground for spoor, but reined back when he saw a shadowy cross on the ground. Twisting about, he stared up into the rocks and saw two fingers of stone forming a peculiar formation that cast an X on the ground.

Sure what he would find but curious nevertheless, Slocum dismounted and poked about in the ground where "X marks the spot." He spent fifteen minutes digging like a prairie dog until he came up with a filthy mail sack. Opening the pouch caused stamped letters to come spilling out. Walker and the Gila Rangers had robbed a stagecoach of U.S. mail and then buried the pouch here.

Slocum held up a few dozen letters, tearing open a couple to get scrip from inside. In those few minutes he pocketed almost a hundred dollars, but this was chicken feed compared to the gold Walker was supposed to have buried here. The Gila Rangers obviously had used this spot before, so it would be plausible to tell the fool guarding the backtrail the gold would go here also.

Walker had not buried the gold here. He had ridden north, probably never stopping. Slocum patted the hundred in greenbacks in his pocket, mounted, and continued on Walker's trail.

Esqueleto Mesa was large, but not so big Slocum could chase Walker all day long and not overtake him. More than this, Slocum traveled faster because he was not leading a horse burdened with several hundred pounds of gold. From the lay of the land, Slocum guessed where the northern trail came over the lip of the mesa, and headed directly for it, forsaking the meandering game trail.

He got to the trail just as Walker rounded a boulder, a stumbling horse loaded with gold behind him.

Slocum lifted his rifle and fired. Walker's horse reacted before its rider. As a result, Slocum's slug caught the horse high in the chest as it reared. The horse collapsed, throwing Walker to the ground. The outlaw scrambled away, tearing at his six-shooter to pull it free.

Slocum got off two more shots before the rifle magazine came up empty. He tossed the rifle aside, drew his six-shooter, and went hunting for the leader of the Gila Rangers.

"Come on out, Walker. Give up. You can't get away now. Yarrow and his deputies are on the way!"

"Yarrow's dead. I saw Reilly gun him down. Never could trust that son of a bitch. We rode together and he turned me in for the reward!"

A slug ricocheted off a rock at Slocum's feet. He took cover, then began circling to outflank Walker.

"It don't have to be this way, Slocum. We can split the gold. There's plenty for two of us. I reckon you done upped and killed the men I left to guard my trail."

Slocum kept moving, every nerve vibrating with tension. His grip on the ebony-handled Colt turned slippery with sweat, but he knew where Walker hid. The man kept spouting off, making fool claims about them divvying up the gold. Slocum would never let him go after he and his boys had gutshot Tolliver and made his own life hell.

"That much gold'll go a long way down south, Slocum. We don't have to worry about Hardeen. I got him in my hip pocket. We can ride back through Neutral, get supplies, and go into Mexico." Walker rose from hiding, peering out toward where Slocum had been. The way Walker held his six-gun told Slocum there could only be one ending.

He came up behind Walker.

Something gave him away. A stone under his boot. A shadow. Maybe the smell of the lingering tobacco. Whatever it was, Walker whipped around, firing as he came. He fanned the hammer with his left hand as his right clutched the deadly six-shooter, firing at what he thought was John Slocum's body.

He missed. Slocum didn't.

18

Slocum stared at the gold weighing down the exhausted packhorse. More gold than he had ever thought of having, and it was all his. All his. True, the army would chase him to the ends of the earth to get it back, but they wouldn't know he was the thief. Enough people around Neutral would identify Walker and the Gila Rangers as the culprits. If Yarrow was still alive, he would think Reilly had been in cahoots with the Gila Rangers.

And Sheriff Hardeen was a good suspect too. The deputies riding with Yarrow would return from fighting the Apaches and know the sheriff had been watched with Yarrow's eagle eye.

Nowhere did the name John Slocum come into it. He could ride off with the gold and live out his days as a rich man.

He could even contact Tolliver—and Grace—once he got settled down in Mexico. Jalisco was supposed to be a congenial spot for men on the run. With enough gold, he could buy himself a hacienda and hire a dozen servants.

Slocum had more than enough gold.

He cinched up the diamond hitch a bit tighter, grabbed

the horse's reins, and walked the tired beast back across Esqueleto Mesa, giving his own horse a rest. Then he rode down the steep trail off the mesa, past the spot where he had looted Walker's stash of greenbacks, and out onto the desert.

By now it was getting toward sundown, and a chill wind blew in his face. He pulled up his collar and tugged at the floppy brim of his black hat, but kept moving. Always moving.

Toward Neutral.

It was almost ten o'clock when he rode into the town. The usual frivolity was muted tonight. Slocum reckoned more than a few townsfolk had died fighting off the Apaches. Or maybe the saloon keepers had run out of whiskey. Whatever the reason, Neutral was well nigh a ghost town. He dismounted in front of the sheriff's office.

He went inside, wondering what he would find. Slocum was only slightly surprised to find a heavily bandaged Marshal Yarrow sitting in the sheriff's chair.

"Slocum?" Yarrow started to say something more, but was at a loss for words.

"It's me," Slocum said, collapsing into the only other chair in the office. "Where's Hardeen?"

"Locked up. He told me everything when I got to interrogating him," Yarrow said. "He knew how mad I was at being shot up. I thought Reilly was in cahoots with Walker, but—"

"But Walker killed Reilly. Or the Gila Rangers with him did." Slocum felt a tiredness settling on him as if he were ready for the grave. Giving up so much gold might have been part of it, but he knew it was more. There had been time to think on the way back to town, and he had put everything together.

"Walker got away clean," Yarrow said. "Didn't he?"

Slocum shook his head. For a moment he closed his eyes and experienced exhaustion from riding and shooting and killing too much these past few days. Then energy flooded back into his tired body.

"The gold's outside. Walker's buzzard bait up on Esqueleto Mesa, if you got the men to go after him. There's another of his men at the bottom of a gully. 'Fraid another got away."

"Got away?" pointedly asked Yarrow. "Never mind. You tellin' me you brought back *all* the gold?"

"Unless Walker stashed some of it, and I don't think he had time to," Slocum said. "The army's got the funds necessary to fight Apaches for another year."

"That's good, real good," said Yarrow. "They took quite a beating. For all that, so'd my posse. The colonel commanding Fort Carleton sent a company to help out. Chased off the Apaches following some war chief named Crooked Finger. A real firebrand, that one."

Slocum said nothing.

Yarrow laughed and slapped the desk with his good hand. "You brought back the gold?" He said it as if he did not believe it.

"You might want to get it somewhere safe."

"The bank's as good as any place."

"You know the vault combination?"

"Miss Reilly does."

"Where is she? I lost track of her during the commotion."

"She's fine. Saw her not an hour ago. She's probably up the hill in that fine house of hers."

"Don't go bothering her," Slocum said. "Put the gold in one of the jail cells for safekeeping. Hell, put it in with Hardeen. That ought to be punishment enough for him."

"You've got a wicked sense of humor, Slocum. I like that. I *will* put it in with him, so's to see what he might have had if he and Walker had been able to split the booty."

Slocum got to his feet. "You hurt bad?"

"Nothing I can't live with. Dr. Martin says my arm'll be stiff the rest of my life, if I live that long." Yarrow smiled. "You ought to get a reward for returning the gold. I'll see to it, Slocum. You deserve something for all your trouble."

"Buy me another drink, after I catch up on my sleep," Slocum said. He left the federal marshal, and wondered what the lawman would say about taking a few minutes out of the chase to rifle through U.S. mail and steal the money in those letters. Slocum quickly forgot about it. Let Yarrow talk about a reward. He doubted he would stay around Neutral long enough to collect.

Slocum rode up the road to Grace's two-story house situated on the top of the hill overlooking town. A fitting place for a banker to live. A man could sit on the front porch and gloat over owning all the mortgages in Neutral. Slocum wondered if Seamus Reilly ever did that. Probably. He was cut from the same cloth as his crook of a brother, Matthew.

Slocum led his horse around to the barn and made sure it had water and feed, then went up on the front porch and knocked. He heard Grace stirring inside. She peered out through the lace curtains, then hurriedly opened the door.

"John!" she cried, throwing her arms around his neck and kissing him. "I thought you were dead!"

"What gave you that notion?" he asked.

"You disappeared after the shooting, the robbery, the Apaches, the—"

He silenced her torrent of words with a kiss. For a moment, she stood in the circle of his arms as stiff as a board. Then Grace relaxed. The redhead returned his kiss with more passion than he had imagined could be locked up in such a trim, petite body.

"I want you, John. Now!"

"I'm mighty tired."

"Then you can go to sleep, but your friend'll come out so I can show how much I care that you're back safely." She fumbled at his belt and loosened it. The gun fell to the floor with a thud. Grace quickly unbuttoned the front of his jeans and pulled out his manhood, already jerking to its full length.

"See?" she said. She dropped to her knees and licked and kissed until Slocum moaned.

He reached down and caught the red-haired beauty under her arms, lifting her up to stand. Then he swept her off her feet and carried her upstairs. There was no need to be uncomfortable when Grace had an empty full-sized bed waiting for them.

Slocum and Grace sank to the bed, their fingers working. He got her naked first, her nightgown held together only by clever ribbons and an occasional button. She worked more diligently, and finally they sank back on the bed. Slocum's hands roved gently over the lovely woman's creamy flesh, finding nooks and crannies to explore and giving her increasing delight.

"Oh, oh, John, that feels so good!" she cooed. Then she gasped as a finger drove deep into her heated interior. Grace lay on her back. Her legs came up of their own accord. And Slocum could resist the urgings deep within his loins no longer.

Rolling over, he positioned himself between her milky thighs. She reached down and ran her fingers through his hair, stroking, coaxing. He bent forward and licked at her breasts, suckling like a newborn calf, pulling first one and then the other nipple into his mouth. He gnawed gently, and Grace thrashed about beneath him as her passions grew to match his.

"I need you, John. Don't toy with me any longer. Do it, please, oh, *oh*!"

He swarmed up her body, kissing here and there as he went. He caught the lobe of her ear between his teeth and bit down lightly as his hips levered forward. He sank balls-deep into her seething interior. For a moment, he thought he was paralyzed. Unable to move, he could only revel in the intense carnal pleasure of being entirely surrounded by a clinging sheath of female flesh.

Then he recovered and drew back slowly. Every inch seemed to take an hour. The deliberate movement stirred both of them to the breaking point. When only the thick head of his manhood rested within her nether lips, he paused to let Grace prepare, to anticipate what he was going to do, then rushed forward to give even more delight than she expected. Over and over, he repeated this slow withdrawal and rapid reinsertion.

The heat from her body threatened to melt him. He moved faster. Her clutching, clawing fingers and lustful moans and the way her breasts bobbed about all excited him more. He moved faster still, until his hips developed a mind of their own. Slocum's brain detached from his body, from his emotions, and he was lost in a wonderland of pure sensation that could not be denied.

In the dim distance he heard Grace crying out her passion as she bucked and thrashed about under him. Her hips lifted off the bed and ground down fiercely into his. She gasped and shuddered and fell back. He moved like a fleshy piston in the well-oiled slit until he spilled his seed.

Grace gasped and clawed at his back again as she came once more. Then they lay in one another's arms, sweating and tired and as content as they could be.

"Thank you, John," Grace whispered in his ear. "You are the most special man I've ever met." Then she kissed him lightly and her hand rested on his chest.

He drifted off to sleep with the woman next to him in bed. When he awoke, warm sunlight slanted through the bedroom windows. Slocum was not too surprised when he saw that he was not only alone in bed, but in the house as well.

Grace Reilly was gone.

19

Slocum took his time fixing breakfast from Grace's pantry. It had been a spell since he'd had a decent meal. Finishing it, he left the dirty dishes on the table. He doubted anyone would notice or care. The house was abandoned as of last night, her clothing gone from the wardrobe in the bedroom. Slocum picked up his gunbelt, abandoned so readily near the front door, and strapped it on. The heavy weight at his left side was comforting, almost an antidote to the bitterness he felt about being right about Grace.

Truth was, he had been right about most everything. It had taken him this long to convince himself.

Slocum went to the barn, saddled his horse, and considered taking the back trail, then turned and went down into Neutral. He was leaving all this behind, and he wanted to take what he could. Slocum stopped at the sheriff's office.

Marshal Yarrow stuck his head out. The lawman smiled at him.

"Top of the morning, Slocum."

"You're mighty chipper, Marshal. All your prisoners confess?"

"Something like that. I reckon I know why you came by." The marshal ducked back into the sheriff's office, then came back with a brown envelope. He handed it up to Slocum, wincing a little as he stretched. His wounds would take a powerful long time to heal. Slocum saw that Dr. Martin was probably right. Yarrow would have a stiff arm the rest of his life.

"How much?" Slocum asked, tucking the envelope into his saddlebags.

"You're not going to count it?" This surprised Yarrow.

"No reason," Slocum said. If Yarrow kept some of the reward money for recovering the army's gold, so be it. Slocum would never know. Anything he got was that much to the good.

"A hundred dollars," Yarrow said.

"Thanks," was all Slocum said. He touched the brim of his hat, turned his horse, and started west along the Gila Road. He left Yarrow openmouthed at the sudden departure, but this was the way Slocum wanted it. No reason to make a big deal out of leaving Neutral.

He had other fish to fry.

"Where'd Grace say that spring was?" he muttered to himself as he rode along the road. In the distance a huge pillar of dust followed the Butterfield Stagecoach. More mail, maybe another strongbox filled with scrip and gold. But Slocum was not interested in such easy pickings. Robbing the stage was a fool's errand when he had a pile of gold to claim. Gold *and* greenbacks.

It had bothered him for quite a while how Walker and the Gila Rangers had opened the bank vault and stolen the miners' gold intended for shipment from Neutral. The truth was obvious, after Slocum stopped making assumptions about Walker—and about Grace Reilly.

Walker had not stolen the gold. Grace had. The safe had been opened by someone who knew the combination. From the way he had acted, Matthew Reilly had not stolen the gold. If he had, he would have left town right away. He was a bounder and a cad and no better than Walker and the rest of his outlaw band.

But he had not left Neutral. That had gotten him killed trying to rob the army gold shipment. But *Matthew Reilly* had opened the safe then, before Walker finished off the banker.

The two masked robbers out on the road after the captain had lit out to fight Apaches had bothered Slocum a mite, but again he had made too many bad assumptions. He had recognized Grace as one of the road agents. It took a bit longer to come to grips with who the other robber had been.

Clay Tolliver.

Grace and Tolliver had thrown in together to steal the gold and the greenbacks Slocum had taken from Walker's camp. They intended to cut him out of both scrip and gold.

Slocum wondered if Grace had any idea he knew. Probably not. When he had shown up at her doorstep the night before, she had been surprised. The fiery redhead had probably thought he had died chasing down Walker. She had given him a nice, loving send-off, one he would remember for a long time.

She and his so-called partner had tried to cheat him. He would remember that until the day he died.

Slocum slowed, and then reined back when he saw a small path cutting off the Gila Road and heading into the foothills. He craned his neck, caught sight of the surrounding mountains, and decided this might be the spot Grace had mentioned before. Before they had made love for the first time. Rattlesnake Springs. Pool of fresh water, shade, romantic, she had said.

"Romantic," he scoffed. Slocum looked down and saw signs of three horses passing along this trail recently.

Grace, Tolliver, and a pack animal loaded with supplies. And gold.

His gold.

Slocum found an arroyo affording some shade, and rested until the sun began to dip into the west. Heaving himself to his feet, he led his horse back to the trail and then into the foothills. Slocum felt rested and ready to tangle with his weight in wildcats. But somehow, his anger had abated. His partner had stolen more than gold from him. He had stolen away Grace Reilly.

And Grace had betrayed him at every turn. Slocum remembered the way she had nursed Tolliver. There had been sparking between them from the minute she'd laid eyes on him. Maybe she'd thought it was romantic for him to take a bullet in the gut keeping her pa's bank from being robbed. Maybe she took in stray kittens and nursed them to health. Slocum didn't much care now.

His nose wrinkled as the scent of burning mesquite came to him. He tethered his horse, then advanced on foot. Apaches were quiet. Slocum melted into shadows, and made even less sound as he perched on a rock looking down onto the small pool of water.

He had to hand it to Grace. Everything she had said about Rattlesnake Springs was right. Good water. Two stunted cottonwoods giving shade from the burning desert sun. Sandy area where bedrolls could be spread out for a man and a woman to make love. Even a rocky corral to one side where the horses could be penned by dropping a tree branch across the opening.

The cookfire by the pool began releasing more than fragrant wood scent. Slocum's belly rumbled when he smelled the rabbit Tolliver was cooking. Along with it, Grace worked to open a can of peas. Spread out behind the couple Slocum saw a case or more of canned goods in their airtights. Probably peaches and other fruit put up for the trail. They ate like royalty.

Slocum sat and watched. The last of the heat from the scorching sun vanished, replaced with a nippy wind that whipped down into his face from the mountains. His partner. His former double-crossing partner. His lover. His former lover.

Anger surged again, and then settled down to a coldness that Slocum recognized. He could live with the memories he had accumulated in Neutral. Still, it pained him that Tolliver had abandoned him so quickly, so easily, even for a beautiful woman like Grace Reilly.

Slocum wondered if Tolliver intended to steal the loot from her and leave her. Or if she planned to do the same thing to him once they got over the border into Mexico.

It did not matter. It did not even matter when Tolliver drew Grace to him and gently undressed her. Slocum watched as the two made love on the blankets, and found there was only an emptiness in his soul now.

After midnight, the two were finally so tuckered out they fell asleep in each other's arms. Slocum waited another twenty minutes, just to be sure, then slipped down the rock and walked through their camp. He eyed their food. His mouth watered, but he left it. What he wanted was penned up in the rocky corral.

He inched toward the horses, letting them get used to his presence. When he entered the corral, the animals considered him an old friend. He slipped on the bridles for the two saddle horses. The other old nag, the one Tolliver used as a pack animal, protested a bit more because Slocum hefted the packs with the gold Grace had stolen. The weight bothered the horse, and Slocum wished Tolliver— or Grace—had chosen a lop-eared mule instead.

He forgot all about that as he led the pack animal and the other two from the corral. They spooked a mite when he circled the pool. One wanted to drink. Slocum tugged the horse away and into the night. He paused, saw Tolliver and Grace lying together, and knew he was doing the right thing. He doubted they would be together much longer now that the gold was gone.

Even better, Tolliver could not come after him unless he did it on foot. They had enough food to last until they walked back into Neutral.

Neutral, Arizona.

He would never see the town or its residents—or Tolliver and Grace—again.

And good riddance. Slocum got back to where his own horse waited impatiently. He mounted, then led the two other saddle horses behind. He kept the packhorse walking along at his left side so he could occasionally glance down at the pack.

When he reached the Gila Road, he considered heading out to California or even east to El Paso. Tolliver would expect him to hightail it for Mexico and might follow.

Let him. Slocum cut across the Sonoran Desert, found the road Yarrow had said ran straight into Mexico, and took it. Four days later he was in Mexico. A week later he was enjoying spending his gold. And in a month he had forgotten all about Clay Tolliver and Grace Reilly.

Almost.

JAKE LOGAN
TODAY'S HOTTEST ACTION WESTERN!

J. R. ROBERTS
THE GUNSMITH